THE GOLDEN Stiletto

D.E. Donaldson

The Golden Stiletto
© Dianne Donaldson 2014

National Library of Australia Cataloguing-in-Publication entry

Creator:	Donaldson, D.E., author.
Title:	The Golden Stiletto
ISBN:	9780994181701 (paperback)
Subjects:	Detective and mystery stories, Australian. Gold Coast (Qld.)--Fiction
Dewey Number:	A823.4

Published by D.E Donaldson and Inhouse Publising
www.inhousepublishing.com.au

CONTENTS

Chapter One 5

Chapter Two 9

Chapter Three 13

Chapter Four 19

Chapter Five 23

Chapter Six 41

Chapter Seven 51

Chapter Eight 53

Chapter Nine 57

Chapter Ten 67

Chapter Eleven 71

Chapter Twelve 81

Chapter Thirteen 85

Chapter Fourteen 89

Chapter Fifteen 91

Chapter Sixteen 95

Chapter Seventeen 97

Chapter Eighteen 101

Chapter Nineteen 105

CHAPTER ONE

Toni sat sipping her morning coffee at the long breakfast bar that separated the cooking area of the kitchen from the small nook in the informal dining room. Her eyes glazed over as she looked at the perfect view in front of her. The golden beaches lay like a glittering blanket of diamonds, caressed by the soft foaming hands of the ocean as it broke onto the golden sands that formed the shoreline. Her thoughts went back to an hour ago, when she was the only person for miles, as she jogged along the waterline. The serene solidarity of the place was where one could imagine they were the only person on the earth. Now the beach was as busy as the surrounding streets. Crowds of tourists spilled out onto the sand, which stretched from Main Beach to Surfers Paradise, to get as much sun as they could before returning home, to their pathetic, insignificant lifestyles and a nine to five existence to show off their acquired tans. Then they would spend the next twelve months reliving their time here, and each time promising next time it will be the same or even better.

Yes! It was nice to be home. The past two years had been worth being away; transferring from one division to another through the promotions in her job. The only disadvantage was she had never made any long lasting friendships. Once Toni left a department, she left behind any friends she had made. It was better to cut all ties if she was going to get the top job in her chosen profession; no friends meant nobody expected any favours when she got the promotions she earned by keeping her head down and working hard.

She had really missed this apartment and the magnificent view of her favourite piece of Australian coastline. A deep sigh passed her lips as she thought of the first people who had seen this coast and fully understood why it was originally named The Gold Coast. It was surely like a nugget of gold, with its promises of paradise with its long stretches of perfect beaches and rolling surf. Enticing one and all to enjoy their pleasures while hiding it's undercurrents that will take the unsuspecting person, with no more than a tug, into its depths and on occasions before they have time to break away and reach the safety of the beach.

Here on the eighteenth floor one could not see the filth man had left strewn about, nor the destruction of the sand dunes by the sand mining companies or the high rise buildings, to scar the coastline in front of her. Only from this height was its beauty apparent, as it must have originally been so since the beginning of time.

'Enough of day dreaming,' she chided herself, 'I have to get on with my day.' She rinsed her cup and placed it on the stainless steel drainer on top of the sink. 'If all of the reports I have heard are half true, I'm in for one hell of a day.'

It was said that her new boss was a real taskmaster who hated women in his department; the fact that no women had ever lasted a full year, seemed proof enough of his arrogant attitude towards females in the workforce.

She had a little bet with herself that he was 'A woman's place was in the kitchen, barefoot, and pregnant' type of male. She felt a cold chill up her spine.

"But I asked for this transfer and I'll stick it out," she said out loud.

In the last department where she had worked, she had access to all the personnel files of the staff in all areas of the department. It was where she discovered there were several officers due for retirement in this station. That meant the chance of a promotion was far greater in the immediate future, here more than anywhere else in Queensland.

She wanted that promotion.
There were those who had said she would never make it and she wanted to prove them wrong so badly that at times she could taste it.

Standing in front of her full-length mirror, she ran her hands over her firm, slender body. She worked hard at keeping her slender feminine figure, ensuring there was no bulging muscle build-up, while still achieving maximum strength in all the forms of self-defence that she practiced.

Cupping her breasts in her hands, she massaged the rosy tips with her thumbs until they were firm and erect; a warm trickle of moisture escaped into her curly mound. She reached down and placed fingers into the blonde hair that covered her moist private parts, slowly moving them in a gentle rotating manner until there was a gentle flow of her love juices. She then drew her index finger through the moisture, before placing it in her mouth, suckling it like a child would a lollypop.

She took her lacy underclothes off the bed and began to dress, ensuring the soft silk suit moulded over her like a glove, touching, but not tight, in all the right paces. Then taking her golden hair in her hands she twisted it to the top of her head catching it in place with one of her own hand carved coral hair clasps. Finally checking that the seams of her stockings were straight she slipped on her high heels. Picking up her bag and the keys, she headed for the door.

CHAPTER TWO

Toni parked her small car in the staff parking area and headed into the station. A few heads turned as she walked up to the front desk. The Sergeant she noted had not taken his eyes off her as she approached him.

"You can't park there Miss," he said.

He didn't try to hide the fact that he liked what he saw standing in front of him, nor what he thought her profession may be.

"Why not?"

"It's for staff," he explained, his eyes slowly undressing her as they roamed up and down her frame, "and you sure are not staff."

His tone left no doubt what he thought her profession might be.

She smiled sweetly as she flashed her badge, "Where do I find homicide? I'm the new sergeant."

It took him a minute to gather his thoughts. This cute little female in figure hugging suit was the new sergeant. He directed her to the first floor by the long way so she had to pass through almost ever other department. As soon as she was out of sight he buzzed the captain.

"Your new sergeant is on her way up".

He'd love to see the Captain's face when she got there. He had been belly aching for weeks that not only would he have a woman to put up with, but he had laid bets she would be a dyke. After all who else would ask for a transfer to homicide he had kept saying. Only a dyke, trying to show how macho she was, would request a transfer here he had heard him saying on more than one occasion.

If that's a dyke, the sergeant thought, then I'll retire.

Smiling to herself, Toni made her way through the maze of offices, ignoring the looks and crude innuendoes as she walked past her fellow officers. They would learn their places, that she never mixed business and pleasure. Toni heard the captain bellowing long before seeing his office.

"Starkey keep your eyes open for the new sergeant. She's on her way up."

"What does she look like?" Starkey shouted back at him, same time as Toni walked up to his desk. His look said he had not missed a detail of her appearance and liked it. A smile covered his face.

"How the hell do I know? Like a dyke. Show her in when she gets here."

Starkey pointed in the direction she was to go, then got up to follow. He had to see this.

"Captain Elwood?" she asked.

He nodded.

"I'm the new sergeant; and I'm not a dyke as you so eloquently put it. So don't ever infer it again or I'll have you up on charges." She paused only a moment for effect. "Now who is my partner, and what is my roster for the next two weeks?"

"Starkey is your partner. He'll fill you in on the rosters," he answered, "anyone can see you're not a dyke," he murmured almost under his breath.

"How can anyone tell by looks or are you an expert?" she replied. "In future keep your bigoted opinions on my private life to yourself."

With that she turned and almost bumped into Starkey who wasn't quite fast enough, wiping the grin off his face.

"I'm Starkey," he said, trying hard to stop himself from laughing out a loud.

"Well can I have the information please?" she asked as they walked back to his desk.

He opened the top draw. "Here's the roster. I don't really follow it when on a case," he said, "I like to be there when the action is happening. It helps give a full picture of the whole thing." He handed her the roster. "You can follow it if you like."

"Oh that's alright, I'm only new so I guess I'll follow the expert." She put the roster down onto his desk. "What are you doing tomorrow? That is when I officially start."

"Unless something happens in the case I'm working on, I'll be here, going over the evidence I have." He paused. "Do you have a number I can reach you on? Just in case."

Her hesitation was evident. "I'll give you my private pager number if you promise not to hand it around."

"Not if it means that much to you to keep your privacy. I'll wait until you get a department mobile."

"No that's alright; I'll only give you one chance though. I want to know that I only get urgent calls on this line. Only my family has it. I find that I get to many smart-arse calls on my department phone, if you know what I mean."

"Yes I can imagine some blokes have nothing better to do than act their intelligence age not their real age," he replied sounding sincere. "Don't worry it's safe with me."

She looked at him as if she was reading his mind, "Yeah I heard that about you" she said almost o herself.

"Oh yeah where did you hear that?" he asked.

11

"Around, just around," her tone implying it was no use going any further.

Interesting he thought, he had never heard that about himself before, even though it was a fact he never told anything to anybody, about the private life of those he worked with, it was a thing he learnt the hard way years ago. Still she was new so who did she know?

"Now can I offer you the guided tour?" he asked.

"Sure that would be nice," she turned expecting to move.

He pointed to the door behind him, "Out there are the toilets and lockers, and over there is the fax. That tidy desk is yours. That's all. Any questions?"

"No you're all heart," her expression showed she enjoyed his style.

"That's me, one big bleeding heart," he grinned a boyish grin that changed his rugged looks into one full of mischief.

CHAPTER THREE

"Well you've been here for a week now," he looked up as she came in. "When are you going to relax and become one of the guys, instead of looking like a little private secretary?"

"What do you mean?" she really looked like she had no idea what he meant.

"When are you going to dress like the rest of us? Jeans, slacks, casual like," he said with a look that implied more than the casual tone he was using.

"What's wrong with what I'm wearing?" she queried.

"Nothing if you are sitting in an office all day but what if you need to gather evidence? Tackle a suspect even, or bend over? How far will that little short skirt and jacket allow you to move?"

"Come over here and let me show you" she smiled so sweetly he couldn't refuse.

Next moment he was on the floor, with his hands cuffed behind his back. The office was in an uproar.

"That'll show you Starkey!" his fellow officers yelled.

"I get a better view from this angle," the Captain said from behind her; his tone was dripping in innuendo.

"Oh I see what you mean," she said as she helped Starkey to his feet. "I'll shop after work."

"Can I come? Just to give professional advice?" He looked so sincere she burst out laughing.

"No it's alright I believe I know what I'll need and where to shop," she replied trying hard not so smile.

After spending a couple of hours looking around the Pacific Fair shopping centre, Toni set off home with her purchases. After seeing how casually the other women and men dressed she decided that she needed some addition to her wardrobe that she had never owned before. These included jeans, T-shirts, and joggers, stopping only once more after the clothes shopping to purchase some groceries. She headed for the car park and home.

Waking the next morning at her usual time, she headed out for her daily run. The air today seemed charged with an undercurrent of anticipation. This job was not only going to be a stepping stone to a promotion, the attitude of the people she worked with was going to make it a challenge to keep on their guard. Male pigs were always wary when challenged.

The next few weeks proved to be almost routine; she went over all of the files she and Starkey were to work on. Making personal notes in separate notebooks, set up for each individual case. The men in the main were not as bad a bunch as she first thought but maybe they were all on their best behaviour, time would tell.

It was one week later, at two in the morning, that Toni got her first page from Starkey; it read 'Meet me for our once weekly at the High Ho Apartments, immediately. I have a hot hard one for you.'

She saw red and immediately picked up her mobile phone and punched his speed dial number. Before he had time to speak she was yelling down his ear, "Whatdoyoumeansendingmesuchamessage?Isaidurgentbusiness.Notthis!"

He wasn't in the mood to be polite. "What did you want me to say? I have a dead body if you want to slowly wake up and come over when you're ready? Get a grip! I'm sick of your sick attitude to everyone and everything that is said to you. Come if you want or not but don't ever accuse me of anything remotely like that again. Do you hear me?"

He terminated the call before she could get another word out.

She was so shocked she sat for a few moments, stunned by his outburst. Then thinking over what he said, she became aware that all her messages were sent through an operator; of course Starkey couldn't say anything about a dead body, the news would spread like wild fire. After this revelation she felt rather foolish; maybe what he said had some merit. All her life she had had to defend herself; maybe she was always looking for ulterior motives where there were none. Hastily climbing into some clothes she headed off to where he was already hard at work.

After running the gauntlet of officers, patiently showing her ID. Taking all the smart remarks they had to say, the press and sticky beaks she finally stood beside Starkey.

"I'm," she started to say...

"Let's just leave it there," he didn't look up, "now what do you see?" he waited until she had looked around the room before lifting the sheet that had been placed over the body.

"Shit," was all she got out before feeling faint.

"It's okay, just take a couple of deep breaths and then you'll be alright," he said quietly into her ear. "Don't be sick over the crime scene though, go outside and note where you spew up so it's not taken in evidence."

A few breaths later she replied, "Thanks, that was a shock. I'll be alright now."

"Yes I believe you will," he replied. "Sorry had to do it, best way in case you are at a case before me. Coming across a dead body on your own is quite a shock even if there is an officer here before you. You always enter on your own." He was still looking her over as if he still suspected she may faint. "It's how I was initiated and I believe it's the best way because from now on, you'll be ready for the shock of seeing a dead body. Quite different from hearing about it isn't it?"

"I'll take your word for it, thanks I think." Her voice was still unsteady but colour had returned to her face.

"Hey have you two finished whispering in each other's ears? Can we get on with it so I can go home to my wife?"

Before she could reply, Starkey replied, "Now take it easy Billy boy I know you just want to touch this deaden, because it has more life than your wife," he joked.

"Now how do you know that?" came the jovial reply.

"Starkey..." Toni got no further.

"It's all in the line of keeping our minds off the actual reality of the scene before us," he broke in, "his wife is beautiful and you only have to look at him to know he is happy in every possible way. If you get my drift."

"Yes I guess I do," she looked thoughtful, "but how do you know when it's fun or not?"

"Depends on who is saying it and the way it's being said, now let's get back to work before they really start giving us a bad time."

It was late in the afternoon before Toni and Starkey had their report ready for the Captain. Starkey took the hard copy in to him while Toni got them both a coffee. Captain Elwood reread the latest report again.

"If only we could find out who makes the murder instrument. This one is identical I take it?"

"Yeah."

"Get onto the lab, hustle them to see what they know," he tried to shift his bulk in the chair. "Christ the newspapers are going to have a field day when this one gets out."

"Poor bastard stabbed during intercourse, the same as the others. Could they tell if he was with a male or a female? "

"No way of telling yet," Starkey replied, "but forensics is doing tests."

"No neighbours saw anyone coming or going?"

"No just like the others."

"Who found the body?"

"The owner," Starkey replied. "Reckons he was checking out if the tenant was in, as he owed rent; says he found the door open and went in."

Captain Elwood slumped back against his chair, causing it to tip backwards. His large frame filling the chair as if it was about to burst out of the sides, a look of complete exhaustion was permanently etched on his face.

"Told the Misses I'd be home early. Christ! Now this, Starkey you're lucky you're single. Beats the hell out of me why I'm a cop sometimes."

"Not single Captain, divorced. Yeah I know what you mean. She was always saying. 'Why don't you cops get more murders?' Then next minute bitching if I was following a lead and had to cancel plans. You would think crimes were only supposed to happen between nine and five," Starkey replied. "Still I'd like someone to do my washing and cleaning some times."

"Yeah," the Captain replied. "Jesus this is the fourth murder like this in twelve months and what do we know? That hand crafted gold stilettos each numbered one, two, three, four, were used to kill all victims during intercourse. Twice the body had been with a women and one not sure and we're still waiting for the last."

"Well each victim was a male, Caucasian, all over six foot, well built and handsome. Usually a male model or in show business."

Captain Elwood reread the latest report again. "If only we could find who makes the murder instrument. This one is identical I take it?"

"Yeah" Starkey replied.

CHAPTER FOUR

Caroline sat at her desk, listening to the instrument she held to her ear.

"Yes I know you want to wear it on Friday; I told you it would be ready for you on Wednesday." Impatience showing on her face but she was not allowing it to enter into her voice. "Yes I promise."

Carefully replacing the receiver she buzzed her outer office.

"Will you please come in here and bring any correspondence you have with you, Peter?"

She got up and poured herself a cup of coffee from the pot that was always percolating on her bench, returning to sit at her desk just as he entered the room.

As Peter entered the office, she ran her eyes over his frame. The wide shoulders were well developed but not overdone. His firm flat stomach, the thigh muscle so taut against his slacks as he walked over to her desk, carefully placing a handful of papers on her desk. She never tried to hide her appreciation of his body.

It's good to have a man as a secretary instead of a woman, she thought. It keeps you alive and also no catty females flirting with the men who came in on business. As long as one didn't mix business with pleasure that is.

"There's not much here that requires your attention; mostly letters needing the standard replies."

John was careful not to look into her eyes. If she saw his most inner thoughts regarding her delectable body, all 159 centimetres with a crown of dark curly hair, cut short giving her a little girl look and emphasising those large brown eyes, he knew he would be out of a job.

She also had an air of fragile dependency about her, that was soon destroyed the minute anyone shook her hand. It had the grip and strength one would expect to find on a six foot labourer. Owing not only to her career, but to the exercises she did each day to strengthen them, to enable her to have the required intensity her profession required.

She glanced them over, handing them back to him, as she finished reading each one.

"You can handle those then. I'm going to change and go into the workroom. Put only the important calls through, tell all the rest I'm with a client."

BLACK WIDOW STRIKES AGAIN. The newspaper headlines were being screamed from all media outlets

Toni stormed into the office, slamming The Gold Coast Bulletin down on Starkey's Desk.

"It's nice to know my partner lets the newspapers know of the latest murder before me. What do I have to do around here to be accepted? Does the last six months count for nothing?" she paused for a breath.

Anyone else would have taken a step backwards by her ferrous tone but not Starkey; he stepped forward so they were almost touching.

"Hey time out," Starkey appealed. "I didn't let the papers know. And I did leave you a message. Listen Lady, I've always treated you like one of the guys, why would I want to stop now?" the look he gave her would have made a man step backwards, he glared down at her now white face.

"I bet," she replied sarcastically. She reached for the small black box clipped onto her belt. The damn battery was dead again. She picked up the phone reaching around the man, not wanting to be the one to take two steps backwards. She rang the message bureau, after quoting her identification number she asked for all the messages from the day before, noting them on her desk pad. Next time she looked up, the fire had died in her eyes

"Sorry."

"This time I'll accept it, but never again. If partners can't trust one another then they split." He looked down into her face seeing the many different emotions pass over her features. "The sooner you get that chip off your shoulder, the sooner you will be accepted for what you are and not those tight jeans that hug your tight little arse." The gleam in his eyes showed he was teasing her and she only just resisted raising to the bait.

"Okay fill me in," she replied.

"Starkey you get all the best offers," injected a passing officer.

"It's the charm," he quickly replied.

"Starkey, Toni, come in here."

Starkey glanced at Toni, "His master's voice," he murmured.

"You called?" they said entering his office.

"Explain this garbage!" he roared pointing to the newspaper.

They glanced at the newspaper then at each other.

"Neither of us did Captain why would we? It would only hurt our case to build up the ego of this maniac." Toni had spoken first. "It's just a gimmick to sell papers. This enterprising reporter has just latched onto to the fact that the Black Widow Spider kills her mate after intercourse."

"Christ almost puts you off sex altogether," the Captain said.

"No need for you to worry Captain. Unless you think your wife is ducking out on you?" Starkey tried to sound concerned.

"I guess not," he soberly replied "That's the last that she enjoys. Hell Starkey what are we going to do about this?" he thumped the desk.

"Solve this before another murder," Toni interjected.

"That still doesn't explain which one of you gave out this story."

"Not me," they answered together.

"Who has full access to the files, but you two?"

"Christ Captain, anyone passing through the station or the lab," Starkey answered, "why does it have to be Toni or me?"

He glared at them for a moment. "Alright I get your point. From now on all files and evidence are to be locked up and say very little to anyone. I'll speak to the head of the lab and from now on only two people there will be able to work on evidence in this case." He paused deep in thought. "It's beginning to be a bit risky we can't let any more evidence leak out and as you said build up the ego of this maniac. It could also start mass hysteria in the general public. Worse still it could cause the killer to get away."

CHAPTER FIVE

Caroline walked out of her workroom, but not before making sure that all of the tastefully designed benches and cupboards were cleaned down and the precious handmade pieces of jewellery were locked away.

She looked at the clock on the wall and was surprised to find it was now two am.

No wonder I was beginning to feel exhausted, at least I have all of my orders for this week finished. With the exception of the ruby earrings and handmade chains, which were waiting to be shortened to suit the neckline of the bridal dress, the ruby and seed pearl encrusted pendants were to be hung off the chains, for Mrs Bray-Smith's twin daughters' weddings on Saturday.

She could imagine what the affair would be like. Identical twin girls, or women really, having identical gowns, the same amount of bridesmaids each. Why they couldn't have the same one set of bridesmaids was beyond her . Oh that was unthinkable! But the whole six bridesmaids were also going to be dressed identically. It was going to be one big extravagant waste of money, but who was she to judge? And they were good customers. One couldn't have something without the other having the exact same thing. Not to mention each bridesmaid was getting identical earrings as a gift for doing their duties.

Julia's choker was also ready for the Wednesday pick up. Yes in all it had been a good night's work.

She stepped out of her orange and purple overalls and carefully hung them on the hook behind the closet door. Donning her previous day's clothes she touched up her makeup; thankfully her curly mop of hair never needed anything but a cut and shampoo. Caroline headed home.

"Goodnight Bob."

The guard looked up from behind his newspaper, "Night Miss. You work too hard."

"No just keep losing track of time. Know anyone who can make me a wrist watch?" She laughed as she left the building.

That little lady needs a man in her life, Bob thought, someone to make her want to go home.

The night club was dark by any standard. The thick smoke from the cigarettes was almost at a stage where it could be cut with a knife but none of the patrons seemed to notice or mind. The music was loud but the patrons didn't mind they just yelled above it.

At this time of the morning the dance floor was beginning to thin out. In the centre a tall fair headed man was dancing with a woman, whose long hair swirled around her like a cloak as she moved around the floor in what could only be called provocatively teasing. Giving her partner a promise of what a nimble and erotic body she had to offer.

"This was a good idea of yours."

"Careful Starkey or I might think that's a compliment."

They were bent over Toni's desk looking at a chart of all the victims, listed under several headings. Names, Age, Build, Job, Sport or Hobbies, Murder Scene, which made it easier to see the similarities.

"Now what do we have?" He began to read across the chart.

"Victim One: Scott Everglade, Caucasian, height six foot three inches, hair medium blonde, eyes blue, well built all over; he worked out regularly at The Body Beautiful. Employed as a bouncer at the Witches Caladium, a local nightclub. Also he did part time modelling through the A1 Modelling Agency."

Toni continued, "Victim Two: Darken Wright, Caucasian, aged twenty-eight, hair blonde, eyes blue, well built, works as a professional body builder for the World Gym.

Also did part time modelling through the A1 Modelling Agency and has had parts in several small films. The body beautiful did part-time tourist guide." She paused to have a sip of coffee.

Starkey went on, "Victim Three: Aza Cuni, Caucasian, aged twenty-eight, hair blonde, eyes blue. Well built works as a Body Builder for the World Gym. Also did part time modelling through the A1 Modelling agency. All over tan."

"This A1 Modelling Agency must be running out of staff," Toni interjected.

"Or the staff are running out on them," quipped Starkey. "Victim Four: Greg Smith, Caucasian, aged twenty-five, hair brown and sun streaked; all over tan."

"Is that all we have on him?"

"At the moment, yes."

"It seems they all have great bodies."

"Oh lady you're something," he gave her a mock grin.

She ignored him and went on. "What do we know about the weapons?"

Starkey checked the files and read them out as Toni added them to the chart.

"Solid gold, hand-crafted, number engraved into the handle in numerical sequence, a stiletto style blade. No markings to depict the manufacturer."

"Let's summarise the facts."

"Okay, all males between twenty and thirty, all well built, all had all over tans, three have worked thought the same modelling agency."

"Not much to go on."

"Starkey why don't I register with the agency and join the gym to see what I can find out, while you look into the manufacturing to find out who could make a piece like this?"

Caroline walked into the restaurant. The maitre d' immediately rushed up to her.

"Miss Caroline where have you been? We missed you. Your usual table?"

"I've had a lot of rush orders Peter, yes the same table will be fine."

Leading the way he signalled a waiter to come to the table.

"Have a good meal. Please let me know if I can do anything for you."

"Thank you Peter, I will."

Taking the menu she glanced over the choices, the distinctive gold lettering on the cover and for each course. It was so pleasing to the eye, she admired the work. *It's good even if I say so myself.*

"I'll have the Colin a la Portuguese, a large chef's salad, and a bottle of dry white wine, please."

"Yes Miss, straight away."

Caroline sat back and looked around the restaurant. She hated eating alone. That was the worst of being between lovers, the loneliness. The only consolation was work. This was a time when she would produce some of her most famous designs.

"It's confirmed a negative on the idea they all knew each other at least. They had similar taste in clothes, but the brands are sold by any of the better men's boutiques. I've got men checking out these boutiques and other stores between each place of residence and the gym, to see if anyone recognises a picture of any of the victims and maybe remember anyone they were with at any time." Toni was about to say something when Starkey walked in.

"Got any leads?" the Captain yelled.

"Inconclusive; one woman at the agency seems to think they dated the same woman, but she reads the papers so she could be getting carried by the publicity fever."

"Go back again to be sure."

"That's a good idea. One other thing, each guy has been in town for about a year and was a bit of a loner, if the information we got from the people who live nearby to where each one of them is anything to go by."

"Good Toni keep me informed, Starkey what have you been doing all of this time?"

"I've spoken to several metallurgists but no-one knows of anyone who could produce such a fine work in gold. The engraving on the handle is very fine almost like lace."

"Have you tried manufacturing jewellers?" Toni asked.

"No, I have got an appointment with one tomorrow a Caroline Fletcher, she's won a lot of awards for decorative pieces."

"Starkey I want results. Soon."

They started to walkout of the Captain's office, "Oh Starkey, give me a minute will you."

"Did you enjoy the meal Miss Caroline?" Peter asked knowing before hand what her answer would be.

She was the type to put on a full force show if not satisfied. She had done it more than once before.

"Yes Peter," her smile almost melted him, almost "was that a new waiter? He is really attentive. Give him the usual tip will you Peter? And charge it to my business account."

"Hope we see you again soon."

"You will," she was glancing at the waiter, "very soon." With that she walked out of the restaurant.

The eyes of every man following her delicate little tush bouncing as she strode along.

"Charles come here," Peter called the waiter over. "You made a hit there with Miss Caroline. She left her usual fifty dollar tip for you. I'll put you at her table all the time. But beware, she likes everything perfect or she'll have your left ball for dessert."

"Yes Sir, thank you."

He recalled the woman was a looker, with a halo of dark curls and a figure that was firm and perfect and so petite. He would be happy to care for her that was for sure; anything she wanted, even without the fifty dollar tip.

Starkey sat on her towel and waited for Toni to come out of the surf. His thoughts going back to the day before in the Captain's office.

"Starkey I want results. So I've made a decision, I want you to get me someone in the force that fits the general description of the victims and place him undercover. And don't tell anyone, anyone, you get me?"

Yes he got it alright; Christ the Captain had a problem with women. Especially since the time one got a promotion over him. He blames all of them now, instead of seeing it as himself that is holding him back.

But this was going too far, not to tell his partner was another issue, partners shared everything. The Captain knew this. He also knew it could jeopardise the whole investigation, but he wouldn't budge. Starkey was up for a promotion and it was all in the Captain's hands to recommend or not and he had made it clear where he stood on that issue.

A cop that fitted the description of the victims; it would not be impossible, but it was asking a lot of any man to put himself out as bait for a killer. But not to be able tell Toni was an issue he found hard to handle. He only hoped she never found out or he'd be mince meat.

"Hi Starkey." Toni stood before him; she shook her wet hair all over him. "What's so heavy you never noticed I'd got out of the water?" She stood naked before him.

"What? I.." he noticed that she didn't have a tan line anywhere on that glorious body.

She was perfect; the breasts firm and ripe, his eyes went to her waist, it was so small he bet he could put his hands around it. His eyes continued down to her thighs that were well developed but not out of proportion, yet he could imagine feeling how they would grab him if they were wrapped around him in an embrace. Not a scar to be seen on her body, or any other mark, it was perfection. He swallowed hard, unable to say anymore.

"What's wrong with you?" Toni found his eyes cover her like a soft cloth. "You've seen me naked before, for goodness sakes, shut your mouth," she was staring at him, she never expected Starkey to ever look at her in that way, it unnerved her. She hurriedly put on her clothes.

Starkey dragged his eyes away, he knew he had crossed a line that was drawn between them and was unsure if he ever wanted to go back to that point in their relationship again. It had been a long time since he had felt that burning desire so deep.

Hell, this was Toni his partner; not some little bimbo he was picking up. No this was Toni and she was more than a partner she was every man's fantasy; enough of this line of thought, he told himself and shaking his head he stood up. *Oh Christ now she will know exactly what I was thinking* he thought as he felt the tautness of his jeans across his manhood. He looked up to find her back to him so he walked to his car and climbed in.

"Get in," he yelled across the car park.

"No I'll walk," she was afraid to look at him.

"Toni don't be stupid," he spoke softly "Get in we need to talk."

She climbed in, still unable to look directly at him. "Well?"

"Look you caught me off guard. I was miles away and when I looked up there you were. It's just a normal male reaction to a naked body. It's not that it was you, it was just an unguarded moment." He tried to sound normal, "Toni please, you're my partner we work together."

She looked up into his eyes, "Oh Starkey I got frightened. You never showed any sign of my being naked got to you."

"Well normally it didn't, doesn't; it was just I was on another planet and there was this body. It was just a normal unguarded moment. Don't let this ruin a perfect partnership."

"Um okay I'll try. Starkey how come you're not married? I thought you may be gay but I guess you're not."

"Not married, divorced. She couldn't stand the hours of being alone so she took in company to pass the time. When I found out I just walked out; never have been one to like to share what's mine."

Toni reached for her bag and took out the spare towel. She rubbed her hair until it was dry, then took a comb and made the long strands of hair into a manageable pony tail, then held it in place with a coral comb.

It was several days later after the staff meeting that they had a chance to speak again.

Is there something going on with you and the captain that I should know about?" Toni enquired.

"No, why? Should there be?"

"OH, just he was giving you all kinds of signals and half spoken sentences. As if he was trying to hide something."

"Damit, I'm going to speak to him. I can't do this his way any longer. Tell you all about it after I see him. Where can I drop you off?" He had a look of determination that made her feel just a little bit sorry for the captain.

"Is that all?" she asked.

"Why?'

"Will I have time to sunbake if it is?"

He nodded his head. She climbed out of the passenger's side of the car and walked to the shoreline and took the towel that was wrapped around her, she then shook it before spreading it over the sands. As she lay there enjoying the sun beating down on her back, the gentle sound of the waves breaking over the shoreline made her relax.

She began to think it had been a long hard week but so had the past months. Most of her fellow officers were taking her seriously, now. That is all but the Captain; what a pig. He'd done everything to make her job hard. Well she had put up with worse than him, so it was a waiting game as to who could or would be the first to crack

He checked out her unit starting in the laundry knowing that she always changed there when returning from anywhere sandy, so as not to spread sand through the unit, where she would put all the washable sandy items in the washing machine, then hang them out on the small, enclosed patio at the side of her unit. There was none to be found anywhere.

As he drove his car out of the unit car park he saw the superintendent who waved him to stop and was informed that she hadn't returned since this morning. So he decided to go to the last place he had seen her. Driving his car carefully so the unique sound of his engine was as quiet as possible, he parked as close as he could and walked down to where she was laying.

"Toni I love the view, you seem to spend a lot of time working out at the gym, as well as a lot of time in the sun." Starkey's voice had an edge of huskiness in it. Just enough to show he was trying hard not to be affected by the body lying before him

"Do you do everything to perfection?"

"You have seen me at work," she casually replied looking him straight in the eye.

His look said that wasn't what he meant and he also knew she was aware of that.

"How did you know I was still here?"

"I went to your unit; the Superintendent said you hadn't returned."

"I didn't know he was aware of my movements."

"You're joking," he continued, "anyway throw your clothes on. There has been another body found. I thought you might want to come even if it is your time off."

"I really didn't know he was so observant. Sure I'll come with you."

She reached for her underclothes. He found himself staring, as she pulled the small piece of lace that formed her g-string. He quickly turned, before the vision became too much to turn away from.

"It's a shame to ask you to cover up but you can't work like that," he said in the most jovial tone he could manage.

"I'm ready," she said bending to pick up her towel as he turned.

The vision of the small petite rear-end encased in a pair of torn denim cut offs was more than he expected and when she stood up her breasts were just covered by a triangle of lace. He took off so abruptly he nearly tripped over himself in the sand.

On reaching his car, he reached into the back and took a shirt that had been on the floor for an unknown period time and said "Cover up will you or nobody will take you seriously ever again."

Then he went around to the driver's side and got in, starting the car before she had time to put the shirt on, let alone climb into the car.

"Starkey can't we go back to my apartment to change into some more appropriate work clothes?" Her voice sounded as if she was about to cry.

She wasn't but the shock of his reactions to her this morning was becoming more than she could deal with at the moment.

The way he had looked when she stood and dressed in front of him, had her senses on alert. She had done this so many times before but today he was actually looking at her like a man looks at a woman. Lustfully only for a moment, but that was a moment too long for her liking. It changed the dynamics of their relationship making them man and woman; not just working partners.

'What is the matter with me,' she thought. This was Starkey for goodness sake, not some boyfriend trying to run her life. He was just someone who she had worked with; he had been just that, a buddy.

'Please don't let this morning come between us,' she thought.

She had been so lost in thought she didn't notice that he had done a U-turn that nearly stood the car on end and was now pulling into the parking area of her apartment block.

"Well are you getting out?!" he barked.

"Oh we're here. Will you come up and make coffee while I change?"

"Sure, I'm going to need something to get my mind back to thinking about work."

He climbed out of the car and slammed the door, striding towards the entrance leaving her running behind to catch up.

"You know where everything is," she said over her shoulder as she headed towards the bedroom, not even waiting for him to answer.

Less than fifteen minutes later, she walked into the lounge room to find Starkey looking around the room. He looked her up and down taking in the image of her outfit, the jeans tucked into long legged boots, the over large shirt tied at the waist and her long hair still wet tied back in a pony tail. He handed her a cup of coffee.

"When are you going to get the owners to do anything about this mess?" he waved his arm indicating around the unit. "The walls are filthy, if not full of holes; the carpet hasn't been cleaned since it was laid. It's so matted with whatever has been walked into it."

"One day."

"You have been saying that for months now!" he snapped at her.

"Hey it is my place. I'll do it when I bloody well want to and not before."

"Let's go."

He put his cup down so hard the contents spilled out. She automatically went to clean it up.

"Oh please don't waste time pretending you like this place clean." The sarcasm almost cut the air.

She finished what she was doing and followed him out the door. Neither of them spoke again until they reached the crime scene.

"Sorry Miss you can't go in there" the officer on duty at the door said as he tried to bar the way into the room.

Before she could reach into her purse, to produce her ID, Starkey grabbed her arm and said, "She's with me."

She pulled her arm trying to get him to release her. His fingers were digging into her flesh.

"Starkey let go! Will you stop manhandling me?"

He suddenly released her, almost causing her to fall over.

"Baby when I manhandle you, you'll know it."

"Where's the body?" he snapped at one of the uniformed officers.

"In there, Sergeant." he looked at Toni, "It's not a pretty sight Miss."

"It's okay I have seen murder victims before."

She walked into the room taking in everything. The room was typical of rented premises, with cheap furniture and floor coverings. The walls, not only in need of a good wash, but the paint was peeling off them. The body lay naked sprawled across the bed with the knife protruding from his back.

Toni walked around the bed taking in every detail. Here was a perfect specimen of manhood. He would have stood six foot two inches weighing one hundred and sixty-five or thereabouts. From the tone of his muscles, he worked out regularly at a gym. The golden colour of his skin showed he enjoyed sunbathing, and the small shoelace strips along his buttocks, did not miss her inspection, indicating while he liked a tan, he did not partake of nude bathing. It gave the thought that he was a little reserved in his approach to others, on a physical level at least. There was a covering of golden hairs over his arms and legs. He took his fitness seriously but he wasn't a professional body builder, for they waxed every hair off their bodies.

"That's the most interest you have shown in any male I have seen so far. Does a man have to a have a knife in his back to get your attention?" Starkey spoke softly so none of the officers heard him.

"You are sick do you know that."

"Comes with the job."

"Starkey, good you are here at last. As you requested we haven't touched anything," The forensic officer said to him as he looked Toni up and down as he spoke.

"Had trouble finding my partner."

"Where is she?" the smirk on the man's face was almost insulting as his eyes roamed over Toni.

"Toni here is my new partner."

"Come on Starkey. I know I've been away for a couple of months but…"

Toni flashed her ID and her look dared him to continue. "Now tell us what you know about this one."

He immediately became all business. While trying to hide the embarrassment he was feeling, being put in his place by a woman. Who not only was a higher ranking than he was, but was also one of the sexiest women he had seen for a long time.

"Only what we've been able to find out from what is on him. His name is Rex Simpson; his wallet was on the dressing table, untouched, so we looked in it. He works as a male model through A1 Modelling agency, is a member of The World Gym, and has an open drivers licence. His clothes in the closet look expensive. There is some jewellery, not cheap on the bedside table. There is also a little black book that'd be any man's dream; he even rates the players. Maybe someone didn't like their rating and bumped him off." He paused as if to catch his breath.

"What part of don't touch anything" Starkey and Toni both said a the same time

"Don't you understand?" she finished off.

"What? I haven't touched the body," he stammered.

"Don't touch the murder scene you were told." The glare Starkey gave him was enough to make the man cringe. "Can you remember what order the things were in. his wallet? The clothes hanging in the cupboard, what else have you touched and moved?"

"Um everything is just how it was." The officer was so stunned by his treatment. "I'm not taking any more of this," he walked out of the room.

Starkey picked up the wallet and little address book.

"Each of these will have to be interviewed." He tucked the book in his pocket. "There is about one hundred in notes here. Credit cards and debit cards, as well as club and store cards. The motive wasn't robbery."

"Is this how the others were lying?" she was looking at the body "Was anything taken from their personal items?"

"Not that we could tell. Those who had family never reported anything missing."
"Starkey can I look at his address book?"

Why, do you want to interview them?" His look said he thought she wanted to do more than look.

"Don't be such a sick bastard, I'm about as interested in females as you are in men," she snapped. "I just wanted to see how he characterised his entries.

She took the book he passed to her. "Um very detailed descriptions, there is a scale code here. She flipped the pages and in the last page found the breakdown of his code.

"Starkey I think you should do the interviewing. By the look of this rating he has here you might get lucky; for a change." She tried to sound flippant, but was sure it hadn't come out right. "Look at this Brenda, blonde, blue eyes, five-foot nine, size ten, rates her a seven average in one - the S column, and one in the I column.

He took the book back "Be the only way I can around here," he mumbled not looking up as he walked away. "Anyway what good did it do him?"

She stood staring out of the window looking at the ocean, when a vision of a small child, bareley big enough to reach things on the table appeared. The fair haired girl was pleading and crying after a man. He was tall, fair haired, and well built.

"Take me with you. Please Daddy take me with you."

The man looked down at the child. "No you have to stay with your mother."

"Daddy she doesn't like me," she said between heart wrenching sobs.

"Be good and she will," he sternly answered walking away as quickly as he could as if she was of little consequence to him.

I've been good at everything ever since and it's made no difference she thought.

"Are you ready to go?" Starkey asked touching her on the shoulder to gain her attention. "Penny for your thoughts?"

"OH! Oh it's nothing."

They left the room quietly, no-one seeming to notice as they were so engrossed in their job of cleaning anything from the room that could be used as evidence.

CHAPTER SIX

Starkey loved to drive on this part of the coast. He noticed as he was passing through the town of Nerang, that was once a quaint place to stop on the way north, how much it had developed; a little industrial area that offered work to many locals. There was even a large urban development on the outskirts offering local shopping and schools. It didn't seem that long ago he was in this area, but on reflection it was a lot longer than remembered at first.

Continuing on he almost passed the turn off to Canungra, he was so lost on memories. This little village was about to turn one hundred and he bet very few people even knew this sleepy little place even existed. But the most favourite part of his journey was ahead, the famous Tambourine Mountain; an area that with the exception of several areas of urban development, was still as it had been since the first settlers discovered the lush plateau that offered spectacular views of the hinterland and the Gold Coast. The lush rich volcanic soil allowed for all types of produce such as rhubarb, avocados, kiwifruit and flowers.

As he was approaching Tambourine Village he noticed the numerous nurseries. Many of them had Teahouses offering the mountain's famous Devonshire Teas, using the rich cream from the local dairies, plus jams and other produce from the local farms. The main shopping street, still had many of the original stores, which were now craft stores offering items made by the small cottage industry that had developed over time.

There were art galleries showing many local artists and sculptures, as well as other works by other Australian sculptors and painters. On the outskirts of the village he noticed a map of the area showing directions to several wineries, offering tastings of their individual wines along with other local produce like cheeses and small goods for sampling and purchasing.

Offering the growing tourist traffic a chance to take back a moment of many an hour spent in some of the most pleasant surroundings to be found anywhere in the world.

He began to think of the woman he had driven all this way to see. As he turned into Eagle Heights he wondered what it would cost to live here, in these large houses on the top of the mountain. Some appeared to be the original large wooden farmhouses, while others were large brick monstrous buildings without any character.

It seemed that the lady in question was well respected in her profession yet not part of the social scene. From all appearances she had no worries about money, but she definitely was not one of the big spenders, like so many others on the coast.

He thought also of the person who had first suggested he speak to her.
Caroline Fletcher, oh boy was she a good looking woman. At first impression you would think she was so frail and delicate until you shook her hand. It was like a steel vice. He'd hate to meet her in a dark alley.

The more he thought about that conversation, the more he was unsure how she had sidetracked his questions by not giving him any direct answers, and why she gave him this particular person's name was hard to fathom out. He hadn't directly asked if she knew anyone who may be able to help. Then saying that this woman may be the only person who could give him the answers he was looking for was even more peculiar.

The driveway looked overgrown. Almost as if it was never transgressed beyond the main road. He felt like a trespasser as he drove slowly through the overgrown track wondering if he had the right place. He reassured himself constantly, he had been given very precise instructions. Through the entrance via the rusty iron gates, with the large lion statues either side. He wound through this undergrowth, until suddenly a well graded driveway lay before him. The driveway continued for several minutes until the house came into view.

It was a large rambling wooden structure. Possibly one of the original farm homes in the area, rambling vines were wrapping around the verandas like a lover's arms, giving the place a look of being at peace with the world.

The driveway ended as abruptly as it appeared almost at the edge of a plateau, leading down into a deep valley below.

He stepped out of the car and gazed at the area before him. The mountain ranges surrounded the vista with the deep green growth covering the slopes. The air was so fresh here; it almost caused his lungs to freeze with its sharp coolness. That made him stand still and breathe it in as if he had never breathed before.

"Mrs Fletcher? My name is Sergeant Jon Starkey. I rang you earlier today," he stammered, his surprise showing on his face. The woman before him was small and plump, she was not in anyway trying to hide her age or size, he estimated she must be in her early seventies, and her grey hair was pulled back into a untidy tail hanging down her back.

"You expected me to be different?"

"Well, yes I did," he was embarrassed, "I thought, oh I don't know..."

"You thought for such a well known figure I'd be slim, glamorous, dripping in skins and jewellery. All originally made by my daughter."

"Yes."

The smile she gave him was one of knowing. It made him feel he wasn't the first to have such thoughts, and probably would not be the last. She extended her arm to indicate he should enter the house.

"Come in and sit down." She led him into a cool, plant-filled room, and then indicated a settee, she took the one opposite.

Starkey looked around him; the furniture was good quality, but picked for comfort. The room itself had exposed beams and a tiled floor, on which were many brightly coloured rugs, the lively patterns, adding another dimension to the room. All the outer walls leading to the veranda were made of glass. Out from these, one could see either mountain views or man made forests. Plants hung from the huge, overhead beams, as well as standing scattered about the floor. At first glance, it appeared they were just placed, untidily, on any available floor space. It wasn't until on closer inspection, it was evident they had been used in place of partitions; so as to give the open effect, yet still retain privacy in other sections of this very large room.

"Sergeant Starkey," she spoke after a few moments allowing the room's impact to reach him. "You said it was urgent we spoke."

"Um yes. Yes it is," he reluctantly came back from the serene atmosphere around him. "I'm investigating the recent murders on the Coast. Your name was given to me as one of the few people, who may have been capable of producing the weapon."

With that he unfolded the parcel he was carrying not taking his eyes from her face.

"It's exquisite." She reached out then hesitated, looking up at him. "May I touch it?"

"Go ahead examine it." He handed it to her.

"You were expecting a different reaction," she looked into Starkey's eyes "When you get to my age young man, life has very few surprises or horrors left." She picked up the stiletto slowly turning it.

She reached for a pair of glasses on the table that lay between them. Placing them on the tip of her nose, she examined the piece more extensively.

"Yes Caroline was right it is beautiful." Her enjoyment of the workmanship glowed on her face.

"Caroline spoke to you about this?"

"Of course Sergeant! We have no secrets, my stepdaughter was curious if I knew anyone who'd be able to produce such a piece besides her."

Starkey stared at her for a moment; her forthrightness was unnerving. "Your stepdaughter?"

"Yes Caroline Fletcher is my stepdaughter. Oh! Now I see you thought I was her mother and you couldn't work out how, ugly, little, plump me could produce a daughter like Caroline."

"No." His momentary hesitation was enough.

"Yes you did. Don't be embarrassed, everyone does. My husband says its one of the things he loves about me. After a wife who was a beauty and a career woman he wanted an ordinary person who could give his daughter some real values to life."

"I like you." Starkey was enchanted by this woman she took command of a situation, and dealing with it so bluntly, was refreshing.

"Now Sergeant before we get down to business would you like a cool drink?"

"Yes thank you."

She reached out and rang a small bell cord that hung from the ceiling, almost instantly a large woman arrived, carrying a tray, which had a jug of orange looking liquid and two glasses. Placing them on the table she poured the liquid into the glasses.

Setting one in front of each person, she quietly left the room. Neither person spoke the whole time. Once she was out of sight Mrs Fletcher spoke.

"This is made from a mixture of fruits my husband grows, no alcohol. Drink up, it's refreshing!"

Starkey drank some of the juice. "Now to business" he said. "Is there any way you may be able to help us in this case?"

"I've been thinking of nothing else since Caroline first mentioned it to me. There are very few people who could sharpen this blade to such an edge and not ruin the piece."

Her hand was stroking the instrument almost as if it was a loved possession.

"The fine detailed work on the handle, now that's a different story; any competent first class goldsmith could do that. It's referred to as chasing. It's like engraving but as you can see the work is raised or embossed onto the knife, instead of cutting into the knife as engraving is done. But the sharpening that is a different story..." She was lost in thought, her words coming automatically. "I spoke to my husband about it when I rang him."

"You rang him?"

"Yes, he is in Sydney; works down there. He suggested I make lists of my different trains of thought. Now where did I put them...?"

She got up looking around her. As she did, she picked up the sheet from the table where she had placed her glass. It was then Starkey noticed she only used one hand all of the time.

"Your husband is in Sydney. What does he do?" He never took his eyes off her.

"This piece is so well balanced isn't it? The person who made this is more than a goldsmith. You do realise this don't you?" she peered at him over her glasses.

"Yes they are a cold blooded murderer."

"That's not all. They have to know many other crafts to produce a knife with such balance. Let's call a spade a spade. It is only a knife, in spite of the material used, or the workmanship that went into making it. Or what it was used for."

Starkey looked at the lady before him in amazement. He hadn't given a thought to anything like the quality of the workmanship, and how it was made. Only that it was used to kill, and was made of gold.

"I see it never occurred to you that the person, who made this, was not only a homicidal manic but also is a very intelligent and capable person."

She looked straight into his eyes, appraising his thoughts, as well as his facial expressions.

"They have to be able to handle gold pouring, and carving and also have the finesse of a tool maker, to bring such a fine edge to this as well as the perfect balance." By this time she was on the other side of the room still looking for the other list.

"Ah here it is." She hurried back with the piece of paper in her hand. "Starkey are all the numbers not in the same Victorian scribe style?" Noting his confusion she went on "The same type of lettering?"

Starkey looked up, once again taken aback "No I don't believe they are, why?"

"Well you see each jeweller, or engraver, or goldsmith has one style, I must be careful not to discriminate, at which he or she is an expert in that field. The fact that they are different indicates the person is even more talented that I first thought, especially if all the numerals are as well done as this."

She sat down again placing the paper on the table, picking up a pen, which lay there and proceeded to draw a line though names on the list.

"What is that?"

"It's a list of possibilities I drew up last night before knowing the excellent quality of the work. I now know very few of them could work to this quality."

"How can you be so sure?"

"It's simple, I judge goldsmiths' competitions worldwide and very few people make brooches." She looked up pausing for a moment then went on. "Brooches must be evenly balanced on the clip or they fall forward. Knives must have the same balance as brooches; if they are not evenly balanced they will not have the effect the killer would require to stab once only to kill instantly," she explained. "So you see, that makes a large difference in the ability of the maker. So very few craftsman hand make them, and we don't allow pouring of items in competitions."

She handed him a list, it had three names and addresses on it. Her name, Caroline's, and Peter Carter, a goldsmith in New York. He read the list twice.

"Of course I should cross out Caroline. She really can't do Victorian Script Numeral to that perfection. I've left myself on there, although with one arm I couldn't do it myself, but I could instruct someone..." with that she became thoughtful.

Starkey allowed her a few moments. "What do you mean you could instruct?"

"I teach."

"Yes I knew that, but it was more wasn't it?"

"Um I recall a student; she dropped out halfway through the course. Now what was her name?" she paused lost in thought. "No it's gone. She had a lot of promise but if only she'd stayed for a couple of lessons. Then not for the whole of each lesson; if I could only recall rightly..." she was lost again in thought.

"Mrs Fletcher is there anything else you can tell me about this student?"

"Not at the moment." Her face was closed to any emotion "No I can't."

"What does your husband do in Sydney?" he asked again; this time he wasn't going to allow her to go change the subject.

"Sam. Oh! Sam is in charge off the Homicide division down there. Didn't you know?"

"No I didn't. Do you mean Sam Fletcher? I didn't connect the two." His mind was reeling, "Why are you living here?"

"I have rheumatic degeneration of the joints on my left, and the warmth here is marvellous for it. Sam comes up every other weekend and now that Caroline is established here it's not so lonely."

"How long have you been on the coast?" He could feel his heart beating almost in his mouth. Sam Fletcher; he hadn't heard that name for years and now he was involved in this murder; even if only because of his wife! His present wife that is. Starkey's mind was reeling.

"About five years now. I don't make friends easily. I hate the false glitter that one must put out to be accepted. It is not so bad; I fly off a few times a year to judge; I teach and design, although I haven't produced any pieces for almost two years."

For a fleeting moment Starkey thought he saw a look of despair on her face.

"When Sam's here, that's all that matters. He'll be returning here for good at the end of the year when he retires."

At the talk of her husband her features were transformed. She looked beautiful. There was no other description for the soft warm glow that crossed her face; her love for him was so apparent. Starkey felt he was an intruder; here was a woman who truly loved her man; he hoped he appreciated her.

CHAPTER SEVEN

"Baby what a climax. Don't know where you went for a while there, but you can go anytime if you come back with such force."

He lay beside her, gently stroking her body as it slowly relaxed.

"You're good yourself."

She looked up into his blue eyes noticing the question there. Turning so their bodies were touching front on, she began to lick the dampness off his chest, slowly working down his torso until he was once again erect.

She rolled him onto his back then climbed on top, straddling his torso, but not allowing him to enter her velvety depth. Then moving so his hard shaft was against her belly button, she began massaging it with her hands while rocking herself back and forth.

He began to tremble as he reached his peak.

"Baby sink it in deep."

"No let it flow, I want to see it flow."

He tried to move, but her legs were holding him with such strength he couldn't budge her. This only added to his emotions; he could no longer control the fire that was burning within in.

Finally he let his throbbing erection erupt. It was like a fountain spraying forth, a thick liquid over her breasts and face, as she leaned into the stream. Just as he finished she raised herself over his face and with a little encouragement from her hands on her own throbbing vulva she did the same to him. He felt her juices run over his face.

Then collapsing on top of him to devour his mouth, like a person that was starving. He could taste his crème mixing with hers as she thrust her tongue deep into his mouth. She worked her mouth up and down his throbbing manhood; she once again brought him to his peak.

Slowly he lowered his arm until his fingers entered her soft wet inner lips, then slowly he twisted them bringing new sensations that made her twist trying to free herself from his clasp. Only he pushed more fingers in, still twisting until it felt like his whole arm was within her. She felt her body responding the sensation so overwhelming she was sure he was going to rip her apart. When the final release came it was like an explosion had been emitted inside of her causing her to scream out like never before in extreme passion.

They lay on the bed both too exhausted to do anything but sleep.

CHAPTER EIGHT

The maître d' braced himself as he saw her approach. Tom had warned him when he rang, 'Miss Caroline is being a little upset today'.

Oh God, he thought as he watched her walk in. *It's the warpath she's travelling today.*

"Miss Caroline how nice to see you again," he paused his face void of all expression, "your mother is at your table waiting for you." He clicked his fingers, "Charles, show Miss Caroline to her table and present her with a cool drink on the house."

"Thank you Peter," she replied coolly, as she followed the waiter to her table.

"Mother." She bent down and kissed the woman on the opposite side, ignoring the waiter who was hovering behind her chair waiting to seat her. "What is this all about?"

"Sit Caroline before every male in this place spills his food down his front." Her stepmother's mischievous eyes belied any harshness. "That's a lovely little leather outfit you almost have on. One of your own designs?"

"Yes." She sat still not acknowledging the waiter who was still hovering for her drink's order. "I had Isabel run it up though, I don't have time anymore. What do you want?" she snapped at the waiter.

"Your drink's order Ma'am."

"Don't Ma'am me! If you must call me anything calls me Miss Caroline and get me a fruit cocktail, no alcohol." He began to walk away. "No! On second thoughts, put champagne in it."

"Caroline is that anyway to speak to someone?" this time the reproach was evident.

"I tip him enough." She looked at her stepmother and sighed, "I'm sorry I'm so busy and when you called yesterday and said you wanted to see me urgently I panicked. Is Daddy alright?"

"Of course he is; do you think I would wait for lunch to tell you something was wrong with him?"

"No I guess not." she visibly relaxed "Well what is it?"

"Just wait until this nice young man gives you your drink and takes our lunch order will you dear?"

Charles placed the drink in front of her and smiled warmly at Mrs Fletcher, relieved that the tension at the table had eased.

The young teenage girl was lying on her bed crying. Her body shaking with the sobs that echoed through the room. She was such a tiny little thing, her fair hair tumbling around her like a misplaced halo; something about her made men want to protect her. Standing over her was a woman as dark as the girl was fair. She was over six foot in height, slender in frame but gave the impression of being strong and capable of looking after her in any situation.

"How many times have I told you to stop fooling around with my men?" she shouted.

"I wasn't!" the girl sobbed, her voice shaking, as she struggled to get the words out.

"Don't lie to me. Look at your shirt, its unbuttoned, your breasts are hanging out."

"He did it Mummy; he grabbed my arm and held me. He tore my shirt open."

The girl tried to lift herself off the bed. Her mother raised her hand and slapped the girl across her face sending her back onto the bed, with such force the bed moved sideways.

"Don't answer me back. I saw you flaunting yourself. You're nothing but trouble. You always have been; the sooner you're out of here the better."

She could still feel the same sick feeling in the pit of her stomach, whenever she recalled the way he used to grab her, and hold her to him, whenever her mother wasn't around, pushing his hard core against her. The clammy feeling of his hands as they squeezed her small breasts in his hands. The smell of stale alcohol and tobacco on his breath, as he crushed his mouth onto her mouth, forcing his tongue into her mouth. The memory causing her stomach to lurch as if she was going to vomit.

No matter how hard she had struggled, she couldn't prevent his other hand from going beneath her skirt and into her panties. She had soon learned not to clamp her legs together to try to stop his fingers entering her. It only made him more excited and he only hurt her more as he had whispered the same thing, 'Come on, let me feel that little pussy of yours.' As he pressed all the fingers on his hand far in, his hand was pushing her small opening further apart.

If she pleaded with him to leave her alone he would always come back with 'you love it, don't pretend otherwise, see how wet you are?' withdrawing his hand and wiping it across her cheek, then licking the moisture off her face.

It was always the same as long as she was quiet and didn't put up a fight. He wouldn't do more than feel her. If she struggled, the more he became excited and would force her to lay down, while he pushed his hard hands into her; enough to hurt but not fully entering her.

She had learned a long time ago it was no use complaining to her mother. She always believed her latest boy friend and he always said she encouraged him by flaunting herself.

CHAPTER NINE

"You win again Mother. No wonder Daddy is such a lamb with you. You never seem to get uptight."

"I do darling but I refuse to allow anyone to know. Stubborn your father says." She glanced over the menu. "I'll have a Chef's salad but no dressing and a platter of fruit, no pineapple. What are you having dear?"

"I'll have steak medium to well done and a Chef's salad, with his own dressing, and another drink with the meal. Mother what will you have to drink?"

"The same as before thank you," she smiled, almost flirting with Charles.

"Mother behave, he is paid to do what we want."

"I know dear. But we don't have to be rude to him do we?"

"You are impossible" she began to laugh. Her love for her stepmother was apparent even she, Miss Caroline, the first bitch of the coast, couldn't help but warm up when with her.

"Okay Mum, Mother," she corrected quickly noting the gleam in her mother's eyes,
"What is this all about?"

Dawn reached for her drink, slowly sipping, and drawing out the moment. "I had a visit from a Sergeant Starkey. A lovely boy, rather rugged looking, untidy hair needing a haircut, beautiful blue eyes. You'd like him."

"Mother!"

"What? Oh yes, he came about the stilettos that keep turning up in bodies."

"Yes I said someone would come."

"Um I know. But did you hold the one you were shown?"

"Yes, why?" a quizzical look crossed her face.

"It was perfectly balanced."

"So?"

"Caroline, it was *perfectly balanced*. Do you realise how hard that would be to achieve? Not only once but four times?"

"Four times," she repeated. "The stiletto I saw had a one on it."

"Yes it appears that this other one that was shown to me was the latest." Her mother glanced up. "The 'one' on your knife; what style was it?

"What style? Why it was Roman Figures, why?"

"Because this other stiletto was in Victorian Script. It seems each one was a different scribe style." Her eyes hadn't left Caroline's face. She watched as the thoughts crossed her daughter's mind, showing in the mirror of her eyes.

"Caroline each one is perfect, all professional, without fault."

"How do you know?"

"I saw them today"

"You saw them today?"

"I made arrangements with Jon to go to Police Headquarters today and he showed them to me."

"Jon?"

"Yes, the nice Sergeant. He was only too pleased to show them to an expert he said. Such a nice man."

Oh Mum." Caroline shook her head. "Don't try anything."

"No of course not," she replied sweetly.

Caroline gave up. When her Mother had decided on a path no-one, not even her tough loud bellowing father could stop her.

"Mother what about the stiletto?"

"No! Caroline stop thinking stiletto think knives. Perfectly balanced, razor sharpened, expertly embossed knives. Stilettos are only sharp pointed knives. It takes an expert craftsman to produce a knife like those."

"So we're looking for a person who can produce knives of this style." Caroline couldn't see the point.

"Caroline I will explain this as I did to the Sergeant." She paused. "We have here someone who can make quality, perfectly balanced knives. Who can make them out of gold? Who cannot only sharpen gold like steel, but sharpen it without leaving any imperfections and who can engrave and emboss in at least four scripts, perfectly. Perfectly, do you hear me?"

Caroline sat staring at her mother, her face had paled to almost grey.

"I only thank God you never could master the Victorian Style no matter how much I instructed you. You were just too heavy handed on the upward stroke."

Caroline felt the life ebb back into her "Mother there are only two other people."

Realisation showed on her face, which caused her mother to rush on.

"Caroline it can't be Rajah either. The person who made these was left handed. Rajah is right handed."

Moments passed before Caroline spoke.

"Mother there is no-one," she paused, "but you."

The last was barely spoken. It was so soft; it was felt more than heard. She stared at her stepmother with such disbelief, that Dawn felt a surge of love, so unbounded for this daughter that was not of her flesh. The faith that Caroline showed in that moment, was her reward, for all the years of raising such a brilliant rebellious child to womanhood.

"There is someone else who could have been that good if she'd kept up the lessons, but she dropped out. Funny I can't remember her name." Dawn said with a puzzled expression on her face, as if unbelieving her memory could forget anything. Her mind was like a computer instant recall on everything. "I do remember thinking she wasn't using her right name at the time. She reminded me of someone; maybe that is why it hasn't stuck, because it was false."

The meals arrived; they ate in silence neither really tasting the food. Both lost in thought.

"Did you have an enjoyable meal Miss Caroline?"

"Um! Yes thank you Peter. Take the usual tip will you."

"Double it. She was a bear today."

Peter raised his eyebrow.

"Alright double it, put it on the business account. Mother you'll send me broke," she chided.

"Thank you" Peter almost showed the shock on his face. The thought that this little ugly old lady was not only the lovely Caroline's mother, but the fact that she gave orders and Caroline obeyed was just too much. He would never have believed it if he had been told.

Starkey! Where the hell have you been for the last couple of days? I've had the boss down my neck for an update. Now today the Superintendent is demanding a full report on her desk!" Toni hollered down the phone.

"Keep your shirt on. No on second thoughts take it off I'm coming over," he sounded cheerful - it infuriated her more.

"You! You lecherous old pervert," she roared back.

"Go easy on the old will you."

"No wonder your ex wife couldn't give a dam where you went!"

"Yeah she really loves me. When did you speak to her?"

"Yesterday when paging you didn't work. I went over there in case you were sick or something and found you rented below her. Cosy."

"Bet you had a good bitch session."

"No we didn't. But I feel I know you better now."

"I've been offering to let you know me better for ages."

"Starkey be serious. What have you been doing?"

"Checking on some facts. I had a long drive. Listen I'll be there in ten. Have a coffee ready will you." With that he hung up.

She pressed the security button to allow Starkey entry into the building, then the lift button to program the floor required, next she released the lock on her door and opened it ready for him to enter.

"Nice to know you missed me," he grinned. He loved baiting her, the fire in her eyes was brilliant when she was angry. "What have you done here?"

he was looking around the apartment it had taken on a new appearance.

All of the broken furniture and stained carpet had gone, to be replaced with fresh new timber flooring . The walls were mended and freshly painted.

"I can't sleep when on a case. So I do things." she replied. "Only I had to wait until my lawyer said I could go ahead."

"You're lawyer?"

"Yes. You see I had it let through an agent who was supposed to collect the rent monthly and inspect every three months. He got twenty-five percent of the fees to do so. He had the same people in here for two years and never saw the place. They paid at the agent's office." She paused. "Anyway from what the neighbours had been happy to say, and the police complaint record, I was able to sue him for all the excess fees plus damages."

"Why didn't you tell me all this before?" He couldn't believe his ears. The amount of times he tried to badger her to clean up, even suggesting she get in touch with the owner.

"It wasn't important," she smiled, "anyway you like to have a reason to pick on someone. I gave it to you." She ducked as he sent a playful slap her way.

"What're these?" he pointed to the files sprawled over the bench divider.

"All the case files, or copies of them; each murder scene and every other detailed report. If we are able to get a full report into the dragon lady today, I had to read over every detail again before writing it up." She paused "I know I shouldn't have done this. It's against the rules but there is nowhere I can set them up in the way I wanted at work." She paused looking at his face for some sign of what he was thinking. Noticing nothing to give her any idea what he was thinking she went on. "Without the other staff members seeing the latest details that the Captain wants kept secret. I promise to lock them away safely when I go out." She was almost begging him not to get angry. And destroy them when the case is closed."

He looked at her for a few moments. "Might as well get hung with you than let you get hung alone.

"What have you come up with?"

"Come into my bedroom I'll show you," she headed off down the hall.

"Now you're talking my language," Starkey quipped, he followed her, not taking his eyes off her firm little behind.

She went to the computer.

"I've reproduced the chart we have at the office listing all the victims, their descriptions, their place of employment, where they shopped and played. Did you realise all were almost identical in height and size?

Each had a permanent or part time job modelling and all worked out several times a week at the same gym. They all preferred the same line of clothes that are sold in men's boutiques only; none wore chain store clothes, underpants, even joggers.

With the exception of one, all sun bathed fully naked." She paused for breath. "Each had been stabbed with a gold stiletto and if we believe what the lab guys say, it was at the time of ejaculation. Each was taken completely by surprise if facial expressions are counted."

"You have some valid points there."

"I know that, but how and where did these men meet the lady in question?"

"That's what bothered me," he replied. "No-one has been seen with them by anyone. Yet they certainly enjoyed the good life."

"The experts are sure there was a woman present each time, but because of the hairs on two of the penises; they're not sure if there was a male also. There was no small pubic hairs found, and in each case long blonde hairs were found in the bed." Pausing for a breath. "Well what do you think?" She waited for his answer.

"It looks like we've got a long haired blonde running around knifing people."

"Yes but is it male and female?"

"Does the female get the final lay while her partner knifes the victim?"

"I hadn't thought of that," she replied slowly digesting this new information into her thought pattern.

"Well I have some more information to add to this."

Starkey then went on to tell her all the information he had gathered. About the murder weapons, how they were made and the lack of people who had the craftsmanship to produce weapons of this quality. Then they added this information to the composite they were going to present to the Superintendent later that day.

"Will this be enough for the dragon lady? Why do they call her that Starkey? What is she like?"

"Not only is she that bad, mean and tough, she plays hard, both at work and outside." He was serious, "listen Toni don't ever cross her. The amount of times the patrol boys have had to clean up after her boyfriends, you'd never believe. Someone once said she had been married and had kids. Pity them if she does. That is no lady, she is more like a fucking computer with no heart."

"Whoa! What's she ever done to you?"

"Nothing," he shied away. "How about a swim before going in?"

"First tell me what she did to you?"

Her tone left him no option. He knew she'd never give up till she was told.

"Okay I was new here and didn't know who she was. Just another female cop and so I made a play for her. Had her a couple of times, but I was still married and didn't want to be at her beck and call so I called a halt to it. Next thing I know I was up for a promotion and had to front up to the Superintendent and a committee for an interview." He paused. "I was never so embarrassed in my life, her opening words were 'Well Jon I know how you can do in bed. How do you do at work?' I got the promotion which I had earned but for years it was rubbed in that I got it in bed." He looked so uncomfortable. "She planned it just to see me squirm because I wouldn't let her dictate our affair."

"Do you want me to submit this report on my own?"

"No the boss will."

"No go he's off sick."

"What did you say?"

"I said he's off sick."

"Convenient," he said sarcastically. "We're a team we go together."

"Whatever you say."

"Hey that's the first time you've agreed without a hassle."

"Must be ill or something," she answered sweetly.

Superintendent Karen Snide pushed the intercom button on her desk and spoke softly, "Are they getting restless?"

"Yes."

"Well show them in."

The secretary rose from behind the desk, straightened her uniform and opened the connecting door. Then she indicated that the two of them should enter. Jon was struck by the similarity in both of the women in the room once he had shut the door.

Karen had come towards the door to greet them. Each was tall and slender although fit not overly muscular. While one had jet-black hair, the other was blonde almost white. They were beautiful in their own way and carried an air of self reliance.

"Jon nice to see you again. Toni you're new here I believe. Please take a seat." She walked behind her desk and sat down. "What information have you in regard to these murders to show me?"

Toni stood and opened the manila envelope she had been holding. "Can I put this spread sheet on your desk?"

"What about the easel over there?" Karen pointed to the side corner near her desk.

"That will be perfect."

Toni went over to the easel and put the spreadsheet on it. She then handed Karen a printout.

"This is a summary of all the information we have to date."

"Well you have been busy;" she looked directly at Toni, "haven't you? Whose computer is this from? It's not police issue No it's mine." Toni replied looking directly into her eyes, almost defiantly.

"Do both of you spend a lot of time together over this computer?" her innuendo was quite obvious.

"We're partners," Toni replied not at all put out, "we spend as much time together as necessary to get results."

Jon sat back he was quite enjoying the word games these two were playing. It was as if they had been doing it for years.

"I'll look this over and see if there is anything you've missed and get back to you." With that she rose and walked to the door.

Jon followed Toni out of the office. He enjoyed watching her backside bounce. It seemed vaguely familiar somehow, but familiar to what he didn't know. Why was he thinking like this?

CHAPTER TEN

Karen looked at her watch, it was two in the morning. She stretched her weary body. It was time to go home.

She picked up the printouts plus the photographs of the victims and the weapons putting them in her attaché case and headed for the door. The lift door to the garage stood open for several moments before she realised where she was. She had been so lost in thought. Something was not right; it bothered her.

Her chauffeur was dozing when she got to the car, she gently shook him. "Brian I'm ready."

"Oh sorry did you call?"

"No I didn't, I forgot."

"You know the rules are for your safety."

"YesbutIforgot.AnywayI'msafeandno-oneneedstoknowI'mnotperfect."

"Who would believe it?" he laughed.

He had been her chauffer for so long now. He knew her as well as he knew his wife. He knew her husband too; poor bugger never had a chance. He'd wanted a wife and mother for the girls, she wanted a career. She blamed him for getting her pregnant and he paid for it.

Oh he knew what she got up to. It was usually him that got the squad car boys to clean up after her. He also knew why.

No-one would dare say a word against her in his hearing without getting more than an ear bashing. He supposed he was one, if not the only friend she had. Something he'd never say to her face.

"Will you be wanting me anymore tonight?" he asked as he walked her to the security door of her apartment block.

"No Brian go home;" she smiled, "take tomorrow off, I'm going to."

"You're sure?"

"Yes, I've got a lot of thinking to do and I don't need that rabble at the station while I'm doing it."

"You're not sick or something?"

"No Brian not sick as in ill. But maybe sick of all this."

"You? Never!"

She looked into the face of her long time confidant. She saw the concern and replied "You're right. Must be tired. Scoot give my best wishes to your wife. Don't forget to have the day off."

Karen sat in her bubble bath, the jets from the spar gently massaging the weariness out. She sipped on the scotch and thought or tried to think. Something was bothering her, something about the faces. She knew from experience she wouldn't sleep until she worked it out.

When Brian went home that night he had an uneasy feeling that all was not right. He and his wife spoke about the day's events. Neither of them could ever remember her taking a day off. Let alone show any concern about him, or for that matter asking after his wife.

Something was really troubling her they both decided.

Karen sat at her desk staring at the picture on the cork board in front of her. Something was nagging at her, but what? Listed for easier checking was all the evidence that was similar in each case. No it wasn't that. If it wasn't that, then what was it? It's not what is here, but what is not written here. She went over the notes again.

Then getting a new note pad she started making notes about the evidence. Yes that was it, the photos they were almost all alike. Yes that was it they were alike! So much like her ex-husband when he was young. Strange that she would think of him now, she must be getting soft. It was twenty-four years since they had divorced.

She reached into the bottom draw of her desk and felt for a book at the rear of it. As she was lifting it out something fell onto the floor. She stretched to pick it up; it's not only that there is a similarity in the photos. It was the dates; they all seemed familiar for some reason.

Yes the faces and the dates. Why were they continually drawing her attention away from the other facts? She got up out of her chair to get another cup of coffee. The time caught her attention. She'd been here for five hours and still couldn't work out what was nagging her. Picking up the lists again, she read the names of the people interviewed. No-one had seen anything, or anyone, out of order on or before the nights of the murders. Strange everybody usually had one sticky beak. Yet none of these victims did.

The name Caroline Fletcher caught her eye. That was the name of her daughter, even the age was the same; but not knowing anything about her, it was impossible to know if it was her. God I'm getting fits of fancy thinking the victims look like Sam. The name of a suspect is my daughter's. Next time I'll be imagining my other daughter; Toni had something to do with this. Other than an investigating officer and that would be impossible. She wasn't even on the Gold Coast when the first three murders were committed.

She went over to the bookcase. Taking out a well worn book. She opened the book. Then out of the space that had been hollowed in the pages, she took out an envelope and from the envelope a sheet of paper with a list of names and contact numbers.

Then reaching for the phone, she rang the first number on the list. It rang out, she tried the second and was about to hang up when it was answered.

"Sam speaking."

"Sam? It's Karen, I need your help" her voice was a whisper.

"Okay I'll get the next plane. Be at the apartment." He hung up.

Karen sat staring at the phone for a long time. Her face paled as she tried to push the unwilling thoughts from her mind.

CHAPTER ELEVEN

"Hi! Lovely day for this."

Sure is Starkey why don't you join me?"

"Don't mind if I do." He stripped off his clothes to reveal a g-string "Well almost anyway."

"What can I do for you Starkey?" she rolled off the floating bed she was on, to fall into the water. His discomfort at her nakedness was apparent; he had experienced it only once before, and since then they'd spent many hours here in her private pool. It was the place they did most of their thinking. Somewhere one could not be overheard or interrupted.

She always wore the same, nothing, so why was this problem again?

"I want to bounce an idea off you."

"Like what?" her curiosity showing.

"Well in each case the victims were in town no longer than one year. Right?"

"Yes."

"Each had a similar line of work, and worked out regularly at the gym. They had all made a lot of friends of both sexes and invited them to their place regularly. But none of them seemed to have a private life or anyone special. In fact they could almost be known as loners when a personal life is mentioned."

"Right, but we've been over this before.'

"Yet the neighbours, who were so observant and ready to complain about noise, from cars, visitors and music, saw nothing on the particular day the victims were murdered. In fact they couldn't identify anyone, who came or went that day. None, by any stretch of the imagination, had seen anyone that could meet the description we think fits the killer."

"I see what you mean but what are you getting at?"

"Everyone has a sticky beak in their area that doesn't miss a thing."

"Yes."

"But in all cases, whether the murder was day or night, no-one saw anything. It seems a little strange if you ask me."

Beep, Beep.

Toni swam to the side of the pool and picked up her beeper, pushing the message button she read out aloud. "'Contact me at home, Karen.' That means we have to head for the phone."

"Karen? Who is this Karen?"

"The Superintendent Karen Snide, who else?"

"Oh." was all that Starkey said

"Miss Caroline? There's an Ms Karen Snide to see you. She doesn't have an appointment." Tom's voice broke the silence in the workroom.

Caroline put her tools down. Glad of the interruption, the piece just wasn't working out. Her conversation with her stepmother at lunch last week kept turning over in her mind, breaking her concentration.

"Show her into the office Tom. I'll be right there."

Karen looked around her, very impressed with what she saw. Like others before, the feminine yet functional décor of the office was very relaxing.

The soft pale lavender walls. All the furniture painted a high gloss white. While the cupboard doors along the wall were in a soft pink. The chair coverings and curtains were matching, in geometrical patters of white, lavender and pink.

Caroline came through a door to her left. This petite female dressed in a purple overall and pink shirt, was not at all what she had expected. The small woman who looked more like a child, with her hair cut in a short elfin style, down to the designer sneakers, was nothing like a successful business woman, let alone someone in such a physically demanding trade. She would have thought that this woman was not strong enough to perform the necessary skills for her profession.

"You are Miss Caroline?" her doubt evident.

"Yes Oh! Excuse my clothes I like to be comfortable when I work." She smiled, completely uninhibited by her child like appearance. "Tom said it was urgent?"

"Urgent. Yes it is. Sorry it's not too often I'm surprised by anyone or anything these days"

"My stepmother says that about age, but I guess not in your case. Please take a seat."

"Don't be too sure. Caroline I'd like to show you my identification. I didn't show your secretary for security reasons." She passed her identification for Caroline to read.

"You're the Police Superintendent." She didn't sound impressed. "My father is one in Sydney."

"Yes I know."

"Isn't it unusual for you to be out of your office alone?"

"Yes it's unusual for me to be on a case. Do you have the time to talk?"

"All the time in the world; I've no appointments today. Go ahead."

"From what I gather you are one of the two possible people who could have made all four murder weapons."

"So I'm lead to believe, although I thought it was three.'

"Don't be coy. We both know, it took someone with knowledge of several different skills and professionalism to turn out such pieces of art."

The emphasis she placed on the last word was evident that she did not see them as objects of art, more like instruments of hate.

"Okay you've made your point."

"Good now I want you to look at these photos and note the dates on each."

Caroline studied each face and then the list of dates.

"I thought by all of the media accounts all of the murders were at irregular intervals. These seem to be in patches of two or three months."

"So you noticed that. What else about the dates?"

"One is my birthday." She studied the photos again. "Although all the faces are different, at a glance they could be the same."

"Yes that struck me too. Does it remind you of anybody?"

"No." She studied the photos again. "Yes. Oh it really can't be..."

"How long have you been on the coast?

"About two years now. After my stepmother finally gave in and bought a property. I visited regularly. Then stayed there with her until I found a place of my own."

"What about your father?"

"He's still in Sydney and he comes up every other weekend. When he retires he's coming up for good."

"Why did your stepmother come alone?"

"For the warmer climate. Why all the questions?"

Just curious. You are both successful women. Who live rather quietly in comparison to others at your ages and in similar financial situations up here?"

"My job is demanding I like to relax quietly when I can. Don't you?"

"No I'm the opposite I like to kick my heels up when I'm not working." She rose from the chair and headed for the office door. "Only in the face, not in our size and outlook on life, we're the exact opposite."

"Yes father always said we look alike. Only in the face; our size, and outlook on life, we're the exact opposite."

"You knew?"

"Yes I've always known who my mother was."

"I see." She was thoughtful; could she be getting old, or something? Twice in one day this girl, woman, had shocked her. "What do you know," she hesitated, "about us, your father and me?"

Karen sat on the chair that was just by the door. Her legs couldn't hold the weight of her upper body a moment longer. Her skin had paled, showing the shock of her daughter's disclosure.

"Just that you got pregnant. He married you, after the birth of twins, you tried for a while to make a go of marriage, and then split up each taking one girl." She spoke so emotionlessly. "Daddy said you couldn't agree on anything even in bed. He wasn't or isn't bitter. He and my stepmother brought me up to not only be independent, but loving and caring also. So I don't use people to get my own way or so they say."

Karen studied the daughter, whom she hadn't seen for over twenty-five years. The independent squaring of her shoulders, the determined chin, her eyes steady as she was being appraised and not afraid of what would be found by the scrutiny.

"From what I hear, you are more like me than anyone realises."

"Yes you're right," she smiled. "What do you know about me?"

"Since coming to the coast you have made a name for yourself in your chosen field. You have lovers but on your own terms. The same way you do business. Your way or no way."

"Well I guess you've got the right information. Where is my sister?"

"Your sister?"

She stared at Karen looking for some sign of emotion "Daddy won't tell me anything" about her."

"We agreed you were never to meet that's why."

"I see." She was thoughtful. "Does she look like me?"

"No she is the opposite in everything, blonde, tall, slim and feminie; yet tough at the same time."

"Who does she look like?"

"I've never really taken much notice. She has Sam's colouring. My height, no-one I suppose." The silence was almost tangible as Karen thought of what she had just said.

Startling as Caroline asked "What does she do for a living?"

"She's in the force. But we don't let anyone know we're related."

"I can understand that."

Karen looked at her watch. "I must be going." She stood once again. "Good-bye." She stretched out her hand, which Caroline shook. "Contact me anytime," passing her a card with only a phone number on it, "it's my private phone number that's why there is no name on it."

"Thank you I may someday."

Starkey had a day he wished he could forget. The recruit that he had interviewed some weeks before, in regard to the Captain's little scheme, was finally released from his previous duties. He had to be picked up from the airport today. As he watched the man walk towards him, there was no doubt he was the right man for the job. Height, colouring, and a swagger that said 'I'm here and I'm good'.

He felt such a heel keeping this from Toni. There would be hell to pay when she found out. They had formed such a good working relationship. Dam the boss; he knew one day he would regret what he was being ordered to do.

"Here is the room I've rented for you. It's just across from the local nude beach and down the road from the gym. I'll take you there later. I've also set up an appointment with the A1 Modelling Agency."

"I don't think it will be a good idea if you come to the gym with me. It may be one of the places that friends are made."

"Yes you're right. Now did you get the clothes?"
"Yes a wardrobe of them. Do I get to keep them after?"

"If you're still alive." Starkey answered. "Sorry didn't think."

"Don't worry. I know the risks the same as you do. When do I get to meet this partner of yours?"

"You don't. Even the Captain doesn't want to meet you," Starkey answered. "Now do you have your file? I'll take it to personnel and organise the expenses for rent, then each week you send to me, in a sealed envelope, any receipts for additional expenses and I'll see you are fixed up for those too. Make sure you mark it 'Personal and Confidential'."

"What sort of expense?"

"Entertainment, car rental, and whatever else fits the story you're telling. Gym, living expenses. You name it you've got it.

"Now the job is looking better every day."

"Oh yeah, here is my pager number. Call me anytime day or night, use a code name.

"How about turtle dove?"

"Turtle dove?"

"Yes it sounds like a pet name. I just say time and place and sign turtle dove."

Toni was enjoying the day off. Lately they were so rare her tan was beginning to fade. She headed for the secluded part of the beach where she could lie in peace and relax.

Spreading her towel on the sand, she stepped out of the overalls she had put on before leaving the unit. After covering herself with suntan lotion she lay on the towel.

"If you don't turn over you'll burn on this side." A husky bovine voice disturbed her sleep.

She looked up, the strong firm legs spread out were just above her head, making it impossible for her to see more, unless she rolled over or sat up. She sat up and went to reach for the coverall, when he clasped her outstretched arm.

"Don't it'll only make me self-conscious" he said.

It was then she actually looked at the stranger holding her arm. He was buck naked and beautiful. Not a sign of flab on his body, it was toned to perfection. The appreciation of this superb piece of manhood was apparent in her eyes.

"Let me introduce myself." He sat done beside her. "My name is...."

He got no further because she stopped him with her finger across her mouth.

"Shush. Don't spoil the image," she said. "I'd prefer to believe you're David come to life."

"David?"

"Yes, Michael Angelo's statue of the perfect man."

"Oh that David."

"You're new here aren't you." It was more a statement than a question.

"Yeah arrived last week," he answered. "My name is David." The grin on his face was enough to make her disbelieve him "And yours is?"

"Toni, but really what is your name?" Her enjoyment of this game was evident in her voice.

"No really, it's David. Guess my mother had some idea what I'd look like, or maybe it was just a coincidence, who knows," he grinned.

"What do you do for a living?"

79

"Anything that allows me to spend time on the beach each day, and pays well. What about you?"

"Very little and a lot of it. Thanks to my Daddy."

"Oh you're a Daddy's girl are you?" His eyes were teasing her.

"Definitely." She began to laugh, "enough of this forty questions, it's nearly lunch time what do you suggest?"

"There's this little place just along Main Parade that serves both vegetarian and non vegetarian meals. So you can have a choice."

He stood up and held out his hand to assist her. Once she was on her feet he began to head off.

"I feel that you may need something on besides your skin." She tried to sound serious.

"Something wrong with it?" he grinned at her turning sideways to look back at her.

"No it's perfect from every angle, but I'm not sure that others would appreciate it as much as I do." She smiled as she stepped into her coverall.

"Okay then I guess I'll have to stop at the car and get some clothes."

Toni completed her dressing and followed him. He stopped at a sports car and as she got closer she recognised it as a mustang convertible. He reached into the backseat and pulled out a pair of track pants, putting them on and over his chest he put a tee shirt that stretched firmly across it showing his pecks to the maximum.

"Nice car," her eyes never leaving his body.

"Yeah got it with the inheritance from my parents."

"Oh you're an orphan or are there any other little Davids?"

"No just me."

CHAPTER TWELVE

Caroline walked into the nightclub. She hoped here she would find someone to ease the ache she had inside her. The need for someone to love her, was almost suffocating.

As she passed the bar she heard a familiar voice and turned to see who recognised her.

"Well if it isn't the high and mighty Miss Caroline," he sneered "don't tell me you're slumming, or are you lost?"

"You're the waiter from the Golden Stag." She looked him up and down, noting the tight slacks sketching across his groin. His hardening manhood almost breaking through the fabric. His shirt was wet with perspiration as if he had been working hard.

"What are you doing here?" she continued, "Surely you get some time off."

"Some of us have to work two jobs just to get a look at the places that others are just spoon fed to expect," he sneered at her again. "Do you want to dance?"

The challenge was more than she could pass up. "Why not I'm sure you can do something well."

He almost dragged her onto the floor. For the next couple of hours they twisted and turned around one another like two wild animals, performing a mating ritual. Neither one of them noticing or caring what the rest of the patrons thought of their energetic display.

It was the end of business hours for the nightclub and neither of them was stopping due to exhaustion. That caused the almost pornographic performance coming to an end.

They left the nightclub and climbed into a waiting cab.

"Let me take you home and show you what else I can do" he purred into her ear.

"Take me to your place," she answered, "I live too far out of town and I can't wait that long. You have no idea what dancing like that does to me."

To demonstrate she took his hand and placed it between her legs. Slowly pressing it up into her warmest area. It was then he discovered she had no underclothing on. Her pussy was dripping wet.

She pressed harder on his hand. His fingers had nowhere else to go but high into the pulsing mound, He could fell his manhood pressing against the cloth of his pants. Then her other hand was tugging at the buttons of his fly. With her pulling and his hardened penis straining against the buttons, they flew off the cloth. It took all his concentration to tell the cabbie where to go.

Her hand grabbed his manhood out of its enclosure so hard he thought she would rip it off. Then her hand was performing magic on his rod. It took all his control not to ejaculate all over the cab.

Within five minutes they reached his unit. He threw some notes at the cab driver as they fell out of the cab. She was refusing to release her hold on him. They tumble through his unit's door and onto his bed, tearing any remaining clothing off. Without any regard to damage of the garments.

He held her down and forced her to take him in her mouth "I'll teach you to tease when I have no way of doing the same to you."

The head of his hard penis was hitting against the back of her throat. She was struggling to try to get herself free. He ejaculated down her throat almost causing her to choke on the thick warm liquid.

"Now you bitch it's your turn."

He raised himself off her only to suckle on her breasts, almost biting them off. Then he began to slowly work his way down her body, licking then nipping, until he had her warm moist clit in his mouth. Then working his tongue in and out while suckling on the clitoris. He brought her to a climax that no other man had ever been able to do.

Raising himself up slowly he began rubbing his manhood against her. She was more than ready to take him into her moist centre. Marvelling that it could be back to this strength in such a short time. But he didn't plunge into her as she expected, suddenly with such strength he rolled her over. Before she realised what he intended, he entered her anus.

The pain was terrifying, and for a short space of time she lay still. Then as he plundered her, showing no mercy, withdrawing from one concave to enter the other. The sensation was saturating her psyche. The pain turning to such pleasure, like no other, began to fill her senses.

Before long she lifted herself to try to get him deeper into her. When, wave upon wave of pleasure washed over her. She could no longer hold back the orgasm that almost convulsed her.

No sooner than she found the release like she had ever experienced, she felt his hot juices spurt into her. Both of them lay spent on the bed unable to untangle.

CHAPTER THIRTEEN

He stepped out of the plane into a day of perfection. The Gold Coast was at its best and he didn't notice. Walking through the terminal he heard his name over the paging system.

"Hello Brian this is surprise." He shook the hand of the man who had chauffeured him so often years ago.

"How did she know which plane?"

"She didn't. After you two spoke she told me to come to the airport and wait, and not to leave no matter how long it takes."

"What's the matter with her?" Sam queried.

"I don't know," his reply was full of genuine concern.

"That's a first."

"Yes. But I do know she gave me the day off yesterday and drove her own car." Her long time chauffer's amazement was evident.

"She drove her own car?"

"Yes and from what I've been told she was gone nearly all day."

"Then she rang me today."

Both men sat in silence for the rest of the journey from the Coolangatta airport back to Southport.

"Here we are. She said for you to go straight up. It's the same password."

"Hello Karen." He walked into her apartment. "I've waited for twenty years to hear you say you needed me."

"Don't be smart Sam it doesn't suit you."

"I'm not. What can I do for you?"

She led the way to the study. I want you to look at some photos of the victims and dates of murders that have happened over the past twelve months." She turned around. "They were stabbed with a dagger."

"Golden stiletto actually," he corrected; she didn't appear to notice.

"Look closer," she was almost pleading with him.

For the next couple of hours he went over all the case notes. Making his own notes. Finally he closed the files and returned to the lounge where had Karen retired to sometime earlier.

"Any chance of a scotch?" His face was drawn and pale.

"I thought you'd given it up?"

"This is an exception." He took the glass of amber liquid and after a sip, "Mind if I call Dawn before we talk?" He moved across the room to the phone, not waiting for her reply.

"If you must." She looked so defenceless sitting on the settee, looking, like a bird perched ready for flight.

"I must. Dawn? Sam. I'm at Karen's;" he paused, "about two hours. Are you up to the drive?" Silence again. "I'll send a car," he turned to Karen, "can you get Brian to pick up Dawn?"

She nodded and went to the intercom and called down to the garage. "He's on the way." Then walked into the kitchen.

"He is on the way. See you soon. Yes I love you too." He placed the receiver back in its cradle, and then went into the kitchen, swallowing the last of his drink as he did.

Karen looked up, "Do you want coffee?"

"Yes black."

"I know."

He walked into the lounge again, and sat on one of the large settees. Resting his head on the large headrest, his eyes were closed as if in a dream.

"Sam here is your coffee." She placed it on the coffee table in front of him.

He woke in a hot sweat, reached out and picked up the ringing phone. "Hi do you feel like a visitor?"

"Darling I always feel like you." a husky voice replied.

"I'll be there in twenty minutes."

She turned the door knob; he'd remembered to unlatch it.

"Come in." He was sitting on the long sofa, with a glass of brown liquid in his hand. "Help yourself," he indicated to the bar.

She poured herself a drink and sat on the settee. David was looking at her for a while. This was one lady he'd like to have around all of the time. What would she say if he told her his whole life here was a lie?

"Dave what are you thinking?" her voice almost demure.

"That it was a good day I met you on the beach."

"Was it?"

"Yes it was. Why not give me your number. We've been seeing each other for a month now. But only when you want me."

"Davey we've talked about this before." She snuggled up to him, and placed her mouth over his; all conversation came to an end.

CHAPTER FOURTEEN

"Superintendent, you wanted to see us?"

"Actually it was you Toni that I wanted to see, but as you are both here now I'll ask you anyway. On the nights of the murders, what were you both doing?'

"What do you mean what were we both doing?" Starkey was the first to speak.

"You're not suggesting," Toni interrupted him.

"No of course I'm not," Karen spoke up.

"That would be the first time you haven't blamed me for something you couldn't figure out yourself." Toni shouted over them both.

"What do you mean?" Starkey looked from one woman to another "Do you know one another?"

"She's my..."

"Toni shut your mouth." Karen almost allowed her raised hand to hit the other woman across the face, but stopped herself just in time. "Why do you always push me so hard?"

Starkey watched the scene unfold in front of him; neither of them appeared to be aware of his presence anymore.

They stood and glared at each other like gladiators about to begin a battle for their lives. The stance of the two. The way they held their heads high. Their build, their determination, he finally saw the resemblances.

At first he couldn't believe he had missed it. Besides the colouring they were identical, not only in build but their attitude to life. They were all that mattered, each for their own selves.

It was no wonder he felt drawn to Toni. He'd loved Karen. It had been more than sex it was the full emotion and it had wrecked his fragile marriage.

Now he knew why he resisted giving into the temptation that Toni had been. His subconscious must have worked it out long ago. He was just a little slow in taking notice.

CHAPTER FIFTEEN

"Mummy Mummy, Please he made me do it," the child was begging "please believe me."

"Don't lie to me" the woman slapped the sobbing girl across his face "When will you learn not to lie to me."

How often had she remembered that night? It was some years later before she found out the truth.

Not until she kicked Fletcher out. Did he taunt her with it? Daring her to do something to him. Knowing full well she wouldn't.

A woman in her position was open to all sorts of ridicule. She was too ambitious in those days to care about anyone or anything but her career.

She had never even let her daughter know she knew the truth. Let sleeping dogs lie was her motto. Why drag up the past it didn't seem to be bothering the child now. So leave it alone.

"Karen, Karen," Sam shook her "Karen, Dawn is here now we can talk."

"What?"

"Dawn is here now we can talk," Sam sounded so worried. "She's looked over all our notes."

"How long have you been here?" Karen was bewildered. She remembered nothing of the extra person arriving. Let alone showing her into the apartment.

"About two hours we let you sleep."

"Oh thank you." Instead of her usual sarcastic tone, Karen sounded like a little girl
Who was trying to behave like and adult?

"Well what have you called us here for?"

"You surely know that. Do you know what the date of tomorrow is?"

"Do you think that has any bearing on this?" Dawn spoke gently.

Karen never understood why Sam loved this ugly woman. Yet looking at her face she saw wisdom beyond time.

"Yes I'm afraid I do but I don't know what to do. I mean if I'm right. Please Sam tell me I'm wrong, like you used too."

"Karen I'm also afraid that this time I may have to agree with you."

"Do you have anyone you can trust with this?"

Dawn's question seemed to take Karen by surprise, "What do you mean?"

"Someone who knows all the facts and can be entrusted with the rest. We have personal things to tell them."

"Oh God. No. What do you think I am? I can't tell anyone what we know."

"Karen you have to." Sam spoke gently as if he was talking to a child, "I have no authority here, and you can't do this on your own."

She sat there for some time, too afraid to think of anything in case she had to make a decision. A decision that if it was the wrong one, would have such an impact. But worse if they were right. It was more than anyone could be expected to do. Or even ask someone to do.

"Davey that was the best time we've ever had." She kissed him fully on the mouth.

Pressing her body into his, feeling every muscle and sinew of his tight body.

"Darling it was your birthday. You deserve a good time." He held her close to him enjoying the feel of her body heat through the flimsy layer of clothing that she wore.

Slowly inserting the key in to the door he slowly opened it, making sure the tentative hold they had on each other was not broken. Closing the door he began to slowly take off her clothes, only to find that she was in a frenzy to remove his. They fell onto his bed where neither noticed the cool sheets.

He slowly kissed her body from top to toe. Enjoying the warm savoury salt from her flesh. At last he reached the mound of her pleasure, as his lips and tongue luxuriated the warm contours. She withered in pleasure. Still he continued, her soft moans began to reach a crescendo. Finally the release he sought came to her. He continued his administration until she was once again pleading for release. As it came he rolled her over; it was now her turn. She took his throbbing rod in her mouth. Slowly massaging it with her tongue and lips, until it was as hard as a steel rod, and then lifting her small body she sat astride his frame and began to rise and lower herself in the same manner as one rides a horse.

She again lifted herself, this time moving her torso forward until she was above his face. Then she lowered herself down until she felt his tongue and lips on the innermost of her until she felt the release of her love juices.

They changed positions and he plundered her moist crevice with his rigid shaft. As he did, she put her legs around his waist drawing him deeper into her. They continued until they reached fever pitch and collapsed on the bed without the strength to draw apart.

CHAPTER SIXTEEN

Starkey was going over the list of expenses that he had just found under a pile of papers on his desk.

"Who has been opening my private correspondence?" he yelled to the room as he read the report that had been included.

It appeared that the undercover agent had made contact with several people who knew some of the victims. No one had any idea who they were dating. But it was apparent that towards the end they had become very secretive.

This revelation worried him. He had been having trouble getting contact with his man and the so called weekly report and expenses letter was not coming as regularly as it had in the beginning.

He knew that to try and contact the agent in person could cause his cover to be blown. I hope he is being careful he thought to himself.

"Starkey," one of the officers in his office approached him, "I am not sure what she was looking at but last week Toni was reading something on your desk and then left." He paused "She looked as if she would kill anyone who got in her way."

"Thanks mate. That's okay we have no secrets." He said to himself, "except this one," then he prayed that she hadn't found it out.

CHAPTER SEVENTEEN

"Karen for the last time, will you please answer me. Who can you trust that has a working knowledge of this case?" Sam was at his wits end, to see Karen in this state, was beyond all his levels of understanding.

She was so distraught she was almost in a daze. Sensing his loss of the situation, Dawn carefully pushed him aside and gently took Karen in her arms.

"Karen darling, we are here to help. But only you know who we can trust." Gently rubbing her back, "Please dear, tell us so we can ease the burden for you."

She spoke in soft gentle tones as a mother would to a distressed child. Karen looked into her face and saw the open trust that was there. She knew that this woman was the one and only who knew what she was feeling.

Following her instincts she whispered, "Call Starkey. Jon Starkey." She handed Dawn her address is book, not once taking her eyes from the other woman. "He is the only one. I don't have anyone else."

Dawn slowly got up off the floor and walked across to the phone. On reaching it she opened the book at the page mark S and went down the list until she found the name she needed.

Dialling the correct number for his phone first, she waited while the phone rang several times, before it was finally answered.

Her body was covered in lather when she felt someone enter the shower cubical.

"There is nothing better than a little soap to freshen up the body juices" his voice was thick with desire as he reached around her to squeeze her nipple."

"Get your hands off me!" she snapped. "I've had enough of you for now!"

"Oh is that so Miss High and Mighty?" His voice was almost threatening. "Well I haven't had enough of you and until I have, you aren't leavening me." With that the gentle fondling of her breasts ceased and he began to squeeze them until all she could feel was raw pain.

"Get your filthy hands off me, I'm going!"

"Not until I say so."

He then thrust one hand between her legs lifting her off her feet while the other one opened the shower cubicle door. Lowering his mouth he caught her nipple biting it until he drew blood.

"YOU BASTARD you're hurting *me!!!*" she screamed and began to kick him.

This only caused him to raise the hand that was between her legs high into her crutch, causing a sensation that was almost as pleasurable as painful. The more she tried to get free the more he brought pressure to the two places he was touching. They were in his dining room by this time and he laid her across the table with such a thump that for a few seconds she was stunned.

His hand was now a clenched fist. Now entering her with such a force she thought he was going to rip her open. At the same time his mouth was now biting at the other nipple while his other hand was holding her down.

"Scream all you like doll," he slurred, "these rooms are soundproofed. I got this unit for that reason. Now be a good girl and let me give you more."

"You bastard," was all she got out before he slapped her hard across the face.

"If you want to play rough that is all right with me."

He pushed her head so she could see his erection, bending over her to lick the blood that was slowly running from her lips.

"See what it does to me? Each time I slap you I get harder. It turns me on faster than anything else."

With that he hit her again causing her mouth to bleed profusely. She was close to passing out, unsure if it was pleasure or pain that was causing her to lose consciousness. Then she felt her body explode into a mass feeling of sensations like no other she has ever had in the past, that brought stars to her mind. It was the most sensual feeling imaginable. She finally passed out with the sensation.

CHAPTER EIGHTEEN

Starkey was trying the number for the fourth time, "David where are you? Christ why didn't I set up a weekly report time."

Next moment the phone was answered by a female voice. "Hello?"answered a soft female voice.

He was so stunned when he heard the voice that seemed so familiar he almost forgot who hc had rung.

David's voice: "What are you doing answering my phone?"

"Sorry but you were occupied I didn't think."

"Hello who is this calling?!" David barked down the line, his heart rate rose as he tried to anticipate what the call was all about.

"It's me; I know you can't talk but you have to come to a meeting tonight it's urgent, NO arguments."

Starkey waited for his reply.

"Oh I can't come."

"*TONIGHT!*" Starkey roared at him and hung up.

He turned to the others in the room, mumbling to himself that he was sure that he knew who it was that answered the phone but that it was not possible.

After he licked her mouth until the blood had ceased to trickle out he tried to kiss her only to have her refuse to cooperate.

"Come on baby do you want more rough stuff? Believe me, this is nothing."

She spat in his face. With that the hand that was between her legs was forced further into her.

David's voice was thick with motion, "Maybe I should go."

She wrapped her arms around him and began to kiss at the same time pressing her body against his. He could feel her hard breasts, he knew that he should leave, but with what she was promising he was more than willing to put off whatever it was Starkey wanted.

David was trying to think of reasons to justify having a private life. He was entitled to one wasn't he? Even if he was undercover no one expected him to be on duty twenty-four hours a day. Did they?

"Starkey," Karen was concerned by the oak on his face, "what is it?"

"The female who answered the phone I'm sure I know who it was. Nah it couldn't be."

"WHO DID YOU THINK IT WAS?!" both Sam and Karen yelled at him.

"Will both of you leave the poor boy alone." Taking him by the arm gently, "Come on out to the balcony and tell Aunt Dawn. Why don't you just take some time to think while those two get us some supper?" Turning her head towards the others, "After all he is our guest."

Leading him out onto the patio she said gently, "Jon look at this remarkable view."

Karen was about to say something but Sam signalled her to let them go. They headed for the kitchen.

"Why didn't you stop them?" she snapped. "How are we going to get anywhere if we don't get to know what he was talking about."

"Karen you haven't changed. Do you still think that force is the only way to get what you want?" He looked at her as one would at a little girl who was in need of a lecture. "The man has had several shocks in the past hour. Is it any wonder he doubts the truth? Leave him with Dawn, after she has calmed him down with some soothing motherly tones, he'll settle and be able to sort the facts from his imagination."

Once the supper was prepared they called the others inside. All of them were expressing their concern that a half hour had passed and David hadn't turned up. Starkey filled them in on whose voice he thought it was on the phone when he rang David's. This was a concern for them all.

"I think we should go to his place immediately, break in if necessary just to cover ourselves. We can get a warrant to enter his flat on suspicion of him being murdered in case we have to."

Everyone was in agreement but hesitant in case they were wrong.

At last Starkey got up and rang the station; he barked out what he wanted and that he was on the way down to pick up the warrant and also that he wanted the officers he named to ready waiting for him also.

CHAPTER NINETEEN

She never made it to the door when he grabbed her, dragging her by the arm back into the room, towards his lounge. Reaching out she grabbed one of the lamps and swung it at his head and it was more luck than aim that she got him on the side of the temple knocking him to the floor, releasing her as he fell.

"David do something for me you've never done before," she cooed. Slowly their bodies lowered; her legs wrapped around his waist to lock behind him, drawing him deeper into her.

Her soft purring noises indicated her pleasure as his lips suckled her small hard breasts. Slowly his path trailed further down her frame, his pleasure was building in anticipation of his tongue's trail.

His moans were loud as the hot fires that pounded in his head finally got the desired release, in his groin.

She slowly crept over his heaving abdomen, past his masculine pecks, placing herself this time over his mouth. Her long tapering finger of one hand massaged her knob, while the other teased his mouth. Slowly her breath began to become laboured. She withheld her climax until the pain, that was ripping through her, could no longer be abated. Removing her fingers from his mouth, she placed her hot throbbing vulva, over his mouth, so he could partake of her love juices.

As they both approached the peak of their emotions once again. She slowly felt below the mattress to draw a long golden stiletto from behind the mattress, to plunge it into his hot body so she could see the shocked and horrified look on his face at the same time as he began to release his juices into her.

Her climax was better than ever. This was the only way she could get full satisfaction. Easing herself from under him she went into the bathroom to shower and dress before going back to work.

Taking her long blonde hair in her hands she twisted it, then lifted it to the top of her head catching it in place with a hand carved coral hair slide.

She gathered up her bag and keys and headed for the door.